SPEAKER

BOOK FOUR OF THE AFFINITY SERIES

J. S. LENORE

Praise for
The Affinity Series

Karla Renken, *Goodreads*

"Relate-able characters, great plot, easy to follow world in an urban setting, and a great balance of romance and action."

K. T. Munson, *Creating Worlds with Words*

"*Healer* is a solid third novel in that it expertly marries all that has come and been postulated about previously with the potential of twists, turns, and developments to come in the future."

Danielle Zimmerman, *Hypable.com*

Books in *The Affinity Series*

Burner
Reader
Healer
Speaker
Keeper (Coming 2022)

SPEAKER

December 2020

Published by Paranoid Shark Productions, LLC

Indianapolis, Indiana

ISBN-13: 978-1-7358445-2-7

affinityseries.net

To my sister

Contents

CHAPTER ONE

I t's pitch black inside the unmarked car that Cross and I are sitting in. Even the lights of the dashboard have been dimmed or taped over to keep us as inconspicuous as possible. I'm freezing, and though wrapped up in a heavy coat with a sweater under that and a thermal under *that*, I can't feel my hands.

Should've brought gloves, I think as I slide my sleeves over my hands as far as they'll go.

Cross and I have been stuck here all night, and I have felt every cold, dull minute of it like an eon. It's like this stakeout has sucked the actual life from my body, leaving a freeze-dried, wrinkled husk behind instead.

There are a few streetlights fitfully fighting back the still-lingering black of night, but most of the ones along the block are broken. Great for staying incognito, not so great for keeping track of suspect movement. Cross is sitting in the driver's seat, eyes locked on the dark shotgun-style house down the street from us where our perp—a kid named Juan Dominguez who runs with the Latin Kings—has supposedly been holed up for the night. A detective with Organized Crime, Carlos

Martinez, is running the op, though he's been rather tight-lipped about what we're looking for. Other than instructions to keep an eye on the kid and make sure he doesn't know we're watching, our orders have been painfully vague.

I've got my feet on the dash, my phone resting against my knees as I flip idly through my apps, trying to find something to hold my attention without draining my battery too much. The car's too old for a plug, and my portable battery gave up the fight somewhere around 3:00 a.m.

As a distraction technique, it's not working very well.

"You sure we need to stick around?" I ask Cross, giving up on finding anything to keep me entertained. "We've been here, what? Nine, ten hours so far without seeing our perp? Are we absolutely sure he's inside and not somewhere else? Somewhere with heat?"

Cross shoots me a look before shifting in his seat. "Martinez is going to be here in thirty minutes, Phillips."

"I think you underestimate how patient I can be," I grouse, sliding deeper in my seat and tossing my phone into the empty cup holder. My ass is killing me from sitting so long, and no matter how I move, I can't find a position where a spring or some unknown metal object doesn't jab my backside with calculated menace.

"You've been on stakeouts before." Cross sighs. "I've seen you do it."

"Yeah, but those actually accomplished something. What're we doing right now?" When he doesn't answer,

I keep pressing. "Nothing. We're doing *nothing* right now, and there are better things I could be doing besides *nothing*." I lean my head against the cool window.

"Thirty minutes." Cross sounds strained, tired.

You can ignore her, Priya offers, floating up from the center console to give Cross a conciliatory look. *That's what I usually do.*

He smiles and I bite back a retort. Keeping my mouth shut for once, I lean into the space between my seat and the door, which jabs my ribs. I shift until it's only slightly uncomfortable instead of unbearable and angle my body so I can still see the perp's house as well as Cross's stark profile.

Even in the dim light, he's handsome. I indulge myself and take in the planes of his face, the shadowed green of his eyes, the soft fullness of his lips. Suddenly feeling a little warmer, I let my gaze dip and imagine the planes of his chest, the soft hills and valleys of his abs. Before my eyes drift even lower, he coughs, and I look back to his face, cheeks flushing. His jaw tightens, and I watch the muscle there jump before he turns to look at me, eyebrow raised.

"Can I help you?"

I grin, unashamed. "I have a few ideas."

He huffs out a laugh and turns his attention back to the street. "You're incorrigible."

"You like it," I say, my voice teasing but my heart still beating quickly in my chest.

What can I say? The man's hot.

"Yeah," he says, pushing hard against my legs and knocking my feet off the dash. "I do. Thirty minutes, Kim."

My pulse settles into something smoother, softer, and I let a grin tickle the corners of my mouth.

You two are disgusting, Priya says with a long sigh before disappearing from sight. *Let me know when this honeymoon stage is over, okay? I'll be in the trunk if you need me, but please, don't need me.*

Cross barks out a laugh and turns around to look in the back seat of the unmarked car. "Is she seriously going to hide in the trunk?" he asks me, eyes sparkling.

"No," I say with a shake of my head. "She's been hoping this would happen since November. Don't let her fool you."

"Since last year? Seriously?" Cross quirks a brow. "Maybe you *are* more patient than you let yourself believe."

"Not with stakeouts, I'm not." I shift again as my back twinges. "Can we at least get a nicer car next time? This seat is going to be the death of me."

"They don't keep nice cars around for stakeouts," he says with a laugh.

He's not wrong. We're supposed to blend in, to be part of the random flotsam and jetsam of the city, and that means we're in a beat-up, barely starts, piece-of-shit Ford from the early nineties. Marginally better than my own piece-of-shit Ford, this one is blocky with chipping maroon paint and a healthy coat of rust. The inside smells like old carpet and wet dog, though I don't know why since it wasn't used by any K-9 units before it was requisitioned by the Seventh District.

The seats aren't in any better shape than the rest of the car, and I'm half-convinced that the springs have gained sentience and spent the entire night trying to work their way into any possible nook and cranny in my body they can find.

Shifting again, I wince and let out a sigh. "Fair point. Driver's seat, then?"

"Fine, I'll take shotgun next time."

I grin at the small victory, then groan when I look at the clock. Twenty-five minutes remaining.

"We could play a game," Cross suggests. "I spy—"

"Don't even start," I say. "I *will* shoot you."

"Ninety-nine bottles of beer—"

I slam my hand over his mouth. His laughter is warm against my palm, and I glare at him. "I swear to God, Cross…"

"What about training?" he asks, still grinning after I take my hand away. "My Mentor's got me doing a couple of exercises you could help me with while we wait."

Cross's Mentor—an older woman from Kenosha named Donna who comes down on alternate weekends for one-on-one training—has been fantastic. I have no idea where Taka dug her up, but in the three months since Cross's powers manifested as bright, glowing golden light, his control has improved drastically. It's good to see things going so well between the two of them, though it's a little bittersweet to watch him getting along with his Mentor when things have been… tense, to say the least, between Taka and me.

He brushed me off the first time I asked him about Ruth Peterson and her group. Though he claimed he knew nothing about it, something in the way he quickly dismissed the question put my senses on high alert. I've had plenty of people lie to me since I joined the Chicago PD, but I never expected it from Taka. It hung between us until he changed the subject and distracted me with discussions about arranging Cross's Mentor. I hadn't pushed at the time. Looking back, I regret not calling him on it. He's only been more close-lipped about Peterson since, and he's stuck to his story. His eyes, though, tell me to stop asking questions he isn't prepared to answer. I'm not used to Taka being anything other than an open book with me, and it's left me feeling off-kilter and uncertain.

I try not to think about the series of missed calls and voice mails that are cluttering up my phone from Banks, either. It makes me a bit of a hypocrite, dodging her while complaining about Taka dodging me, but in the months since everything happened with Steve, we haven't gotten any closer to figuring out why that red energy is appearing all over Chicago or how to get rid of it. While she's been researching the bindings that stop it from spreading, I've been avoiding anything and everything to do with it, choosing to worry about whatever else I can think of instead.

"All right," I say, dragging my focus back to Cross. "What've you got?"

His gaze softens as he falls into Second-Sight. I join him a second later, watching the world as it erupts into shining, multihued light. It still catches me off guard, the added shades that now make up the world around me. I spent all of my life with the supernatural world outlined in blue-white. Seeing the familiar color mixed in with shades of green and red is still startling.

"Donna said that there's a sensation to each Affinity, a unique signature that can help you identify how your power is going to develop, even before it does." He holds his hand in front of him, palm up. "If I come into contact with the Affinity, it might trigger my own."

"No luck with hers?"

Cross shakes his head. "She's a Burner, and I haven't gotten anything from her when we've tried this. Whatever's going on with me, though, you seem to draw it out. She thought it might work better if we tried."

I think of the warding in January, of drawing runes and sigils against the ridged planes of his body, of light erupting from his skin in a warm, golden glow. My cheeks heat.

"What do you need me to do?" I ask with a slightly shaky voice.

"She said you'd need to push with your Affinities. Though I'm not entirely sure what that means."

"I think I do." I lay my fingers against his palm.

Focusing my power, I let it twist and trail its way up my arm to gather in my hand. My veins glow with it, a shifting light show under my skin. Slowly, the colors still, and as I focus, the red and green fade, replaced by blue-white. I force the energy down my fingers, pressing it against Cross's skin.

"You feeling anything?" I ask, my voice unexpectedly breathless as power pours from my hand over his skin. "Can you tell which one I'm using?"

"Burner," Cross says, sounding hesitant. "It feels… familiar, I guess."

"And nothing on your end?"

Cross shakes his head, and I shift my focus again. The light in my hand flashes fiery red, and I have to fight against Reading him. It hasn't happened since the first time, but I desperately don't want to repeat the experience, especially since I still haven't found a way to tell him about it.

"Now?"

Another shake. "But it's different from before. Which one is it?"

"Reader," I say. "You let me know when I switch again."

I move into Healing, grass-green light shimmering between our hands and coursing, unbidden, into his skin. He shivers.

"Sorry," I say. "Didn't mean to zap you."

"No, it felt good," he says, and when I meet his eyes,

they flash with heat. I let myself slip out of Second-Sight and trail my fingers from the palm of Cross's hand to the racing pulse in his wrist. "Healing?"

I nod and let my fingers coast over his palms, tracing the paths of wrinkles as they zigzag across his skin. "You sure you don't want to do something else? You know what they say about all work…"

He grabs my fingers and pulls my hand to his mouth, pressing a gentle kiss against my knuckles before nipping at them with a flash of a grin. A gasp escapes from me as he soothes the sting of his teeth with his tongue. "After Martinez gets here, we can do whatever we want."

"You're a pain in the ass." I pull my hand back, shifting in my seat again from a different kind of discomfort.

He grins. "You like it."

"Yeah." I sigh and slouch in my seat. "I do. You get anything from that last one, other than a thrill?"

"No, nothing." He looks a little disappointed, and I wish there was something I could do to help. "I'm sure I'll get there, though."

"You know, not everyone does," I say carefully. "Being Sighted doesn't mean you're guaranteed to be a Medium. And considering you weren't even that a few months ago…"

"I know, I know." He rolls his eyes. "We've been over this before, Kim."

"I don't want you to get your hopes up and be

disappointed." I try to soften my words, knowing that it's a sore subject.

"And while I appreciate that"—and his words are sincere, though he's clearly annoyed with the way this conversation is going—"I'm going to keep trying."

"Okay." I'm wondering if I can convince him to make out a little when lights flash on inside the house we're watching. I stop, leaning over the center console, and frown. "You see that?"

"Yeah." He sits forward, and I move back to my seat. "You think our perp is moving?"

"Maybe."

Priya, I Send, and she appears next to us. *Any chance you can do some recon?*

Isn't that against the Fourth Amendment? She grins at me. *Oh, wait. I'm dead. Doesn't apply. I'll be right back.*

I don't know how I feel about your cavalier attitude toward our constitutional rights, miss.

It's your fault, she teases back. *Now hush, I need to concentrate.*

I drop fully into Second-Sight so I can keep an eye on her. She stands out against her surroundings, bright and glowing with power as she moves closer to the house. She disappears through the wall, and I wait, breathless for some reason, even though I know she can't be hurt.

What's this guy look like again? Her voice is hesitant, and she sounds confused.

I pull out Dominguez's rap sheet and start reading

over his details. *Young, Hispanic, brown hair and eyes. Five seven with full-sleeve tattoos.*

Hm. She pauses. *Well, I've got some bad news, then.*

He's gone?

Oh no, he's here. He's just dead.

Chapter Two

"What?" Cross says, already reaching for the door handle. "If he's dead, who turned on the lights?"

"She can't hear you from here if you don't Send," I remind him before stepping out of the car and reaching to unsnap my holster.

Who turned the lights on? Cross asks as he shuts his door.

No idea. There's no one else here.

Cross and I move quickly toward the house. He hurries up the front steps, and I lag a step behind him, keeping an eye on his back. Trying the door, he finds it locked and shakes his head.

Priya, a little help.

On it.

A moment later, we hear the lock trip, and when Cross tries it again, the door springs open. There's a small foyer with a living room off to the right. Right inside the door, lying on his front in a pool of blood is Dominguez. Cross curses, and we both step around the body carefully. There's spatter on the walls and floor.

Judging by the number of stains covering Dominguez's back, he's been shot a couple of times. The exit wounds look clean, and I wonder how in the hell we missed gunshots when we were only fifty yards away.

Cross curses again.

"Let's clear the building and I'll call Dispatch," I say and head deeper into the house.

We walk carefully through the rest of the rooms, clearing them as we go. The living area is dominated by a large TV and not much else. A bathroom and two bedrooms are in the back, located adjacent to the living room, both barely large enough for the mattresses lying on the floor. A small but tidy kitchen takes up the back of the house, with a rear entrance that opens onto an unfenced backyard overgrown with weeds.

There's a broken windowpane in the top half of the back door. Separated by strips of wood, the glass is fractured in a wild spiderweb of cracks. The pane closest to the doorknob is missing most of its glass, the remaining pieces crazed and cracked. The doorknob, easily reachable through the hole in the glass, is unlocked.

There's no one else in the house and no signs of disturbance other than the broken glass in the kitchen. Cross and I holster our weapons, and I call Dispatch right as Martinez walks up the front steps, the door still open to the street.

Detective Carlos Martinez is older than Cross and me, but he carries his age well. His hair is dark, though there's a slight dusting of gray at his temples and subtle wrinkles in the corners of his eyes. Otherwise, it's hard to tell he's been with the CPD Bureau of Detectives and Organized Crime for more than a decade and a half. He's in good shape, his shoulders square and waist trim, and though not the tallest officer in the district, he stands with an authority that gives him more presence than a few extra inches would. Tonight, he's wearing a heavy winter jacket, the collar turned up against the early-morning chill, and his detective's badge hangs around his neck, bouncing against his chest as he walks through the door, eyes wide.

"Well, shit," he says, staring down at Dominguez as he hurries toward Cross and me. "What did you guys do?

"Nothing," Cross says. He gestures at Martinez. "Shut the door."

I explain the situation to Dispatch as Cross steps to the side to talk to Martinez. After requesting resources—uniformed officers for a cordon and canvassing, Forensics to process the crime scene, and the medical examiner's office to pick up the body for autopsy—I head back to the front hall where Cross and Martinez are still talking.

"And then we came inside," Cross says as he gestures toward Dominguez's body, "and found our guy here."

"So, you didn't see or hear anything?" Martinez asks again, as if the situation will make more sense if Cross explains it to him again.

I shake my head. "No, nothing. The house was dark

and quiet all night. The lights went off around ten o'clock, and it's been like that until they turned on a little before you got here."

"They must be on a timer or something." He curses again. "Dammit. We needed this kid."

"Why?" I ask. "His sheet said he's a money guy for the Latin Kings, but I didn't think he was high level."

"It's complicated," Martinez says, still looking at the body by his feet as if annoyed.

I frown. "Why do I get the feeling that we're missing something here?" Martinez looks at me, eyes wide. "Remind me to play poker with you sometime, Carlos."

"I don't know what you're talking about."

Now Cross's eyebrows raise. "That's what you're going to go with?"

"It's early." Martinez runs a hand over his tired expression as if he can wipe it away. "I haven't had enough coffee for this conversation."

"That's not really a deterrent for me," I say, half joking. "Seems like I should press my advantage while I can."

"Why did I ask you to surveil this guy again?" Martinez asks.

"Because of my winning personality and sparkling wit," I deadpan, and he huffs out a surprised laugh.

"I should've known better." He shakes his head. Sirens approach outside, and he turns back to the door, running his hand through his hair as he sighs. "Let's get the scene secured, and then… we'll talk."

Forensics is efficient as ever. We help the uniforms put up barrier tape and wooden barricades, blocking access to both the front and back doors as well as the backyard. The medical examiner is on his way, and in the front entry, techs have already started taking photos of Dominguez's body and the blood spatter surrounding it. Another tech in a white Tyvek jumpsuit is crouched near the back door, taking prints, as another uniformed officer walks through the backyard, searching for any footprints or signs of the person who broke through the back door.

Cross, Martinez, and I move around to the side of the house, out of the way. Once he confirms that we're alone, Martinez starts talking.

"This doesn't go any further than the three of us, you understand?" When Cross and I nod, Martinez sighs. "Dominguez was a CI."

My eyebrows shoot up. "He's with the Latin Kings. They don't snitch."

"This one does." Martinez rubs the bridge of his nose, forehead creased in frustration. "Or at least he *did*. We were depending on him for a big op. This is going to put months of work in jeopardy if it doesn't manage to tank the investigation entirely."

"What are you looking into?" Cross shifts closer. "What kind of operation are we talking about here?"

Martinez kicks at the ground. "I can't give you any more details than that." He holds up a hand when Cross opens his mouth to respond. "I know you're a good detective, Riley. You're solid. It's nothing personal. I'm under strict orders from people way above either of our pay grades to not talk to anyone who isn't already in the know. I'd love to tell you, but I can't."

Cross frowns but nods.

I'm not as understanding.

"What kind of shit is that?" I ask. "How serious is this thing?"

"Kim." Cross shoots me a look. "Let it go."

"No." I take a step toward Martinez. "You had us watching this guy all night, and now he's dead. We're going to look like idiots at best, incompetent at worst. I think we deserve more of an explanation than 'Sorry, my hands are tied.'"

Martinez glares at me. Dawn is finally breaking, light barely peeking over the horizon, and it glints in his eyes. He's a veteran officer, and those long years show in the hard expression on his face, the tired edge in his eyes. I fight against the urge to back down, my shoulders tight as I try to brazen my way through this silent confrontation. After another long moment, our eyes locked, Martinez looks away, tips his head back, and groans from low in his throat.

"I fucking hate you, Phillips," he says and points at me. "You say anything and I will have your badge. Do you understand me?"

"Yeah."

"I'm not giving you any details, and I'm only telling you the basics because you're both good detectives. I trust you, even if"—he looks at me—"you annoy the shit out of me." He takes a deep breath and lets it out slowly. "Dominguez told us an officer is working with the Latin Kings."

Stunned, I ask, "And you were able to corroborate it?"

Martinez nods. "He wouldn't tell us who it was, but he knew details that he shouldn't have known about gang ops that have gone sideways in the last six months. Things that he only could've learned from an officer involved in the investigations."

"Damn," Cross says, running a hand through his hair. "Is IA involved?"

"Yeah," Martinez says, "but I'm not telling you who's working it. They have a hard enough time with all that 'rat squad' bullshit they have to put up with, and since we're still trying to figure out who to look at for it, it's under lock and key."

"Yeah, no kidding," I say. "Of course, you can't say anything."

"And now, neither can you. I'll get the paperwork handled, but in the meantime, I'm trusting you to keep your mouths shut. I've got a fucking mess to clean up back at HQ. Can you handle the scene, work on figuring out who killed this guy?"

"Yeah." I'm still reeling from his admission. A weight settles on my shoulders, making me stand up a little straighter. "Yeah, we'll handle this."

"Good." He turns and stalks toward the front yard.

I turn to Cross. "Guess we're going to be busy."

"I need coffee." He cracks his back, and I wince at the sound. "Let's get to work, partner."

"You take the back of the house, I'll take the front?"

He nods. "Flag down a uniform. See if you can get some coffee here."

As I round the front corner of the house, he calls my name.

"No sugar."

"Just cream," I say with a roll of my eyes. "I know your coffee order, Cross."

He grins. "I know, but I like hearing it."

"Get to work, Detective." I laugh. "I'll get you when the medical examiner arrives or if I find anything interesting."

I walk into the front yard of the house and scan the street. Other houses in the same style as the crime scene stand shoulder to shoulder, their thin side yards just large enough for a person to walk through comfortably. While we've secured the scene, a few lights have turned on, but the neighbors are keeping to themselves. Some peek through their curtains, yet none open their doors to take in the flashing lights and hive of police activity around the house. Part of me thinks they might be used to it, the signs of early-morning violence and disruption that come with a crime. Another part wonders if they simply don't want to get dragged into trouble.

Either way, I have a feeling that we won't find any witnesses, especially since Cross and I were parked down the street all night and didn't see a damn thing.

Whoever killed Dominguez probably came up from another block, cutting through the backyard before breaking in via the back door.

I head up the front steps. Taking in the yellow crime scene markers spread around the front entry and the giant bloodstain spread around Dominguez's body, I carefully walk inside and turn to one of the techs.

"You find any of the bullets?" I ask, looking at the front wall of the house where there are four dark circles with bright yellow identifying markers.

"Yes, Detective," the woman says, her hair hidden by the Tyvek suit she's wearing. "We've got four points of impact on that back wall. Still need to calculate trajectory and try to retrieve the bullets."

"No casings?"

"No, ma'am. The shooter may have taken them when they left the scene."

"Thank you." I move around her to stand a few feet away from the body, positioning myself as if I had approached Dominguez from behind. I raise my arm, pointing my finger like a gun, and imagine the killer coming up behind Dominguez, gun raised and firing.

"Do you mind?" I ask as I move closer to the body. When the tech shakes her head and moves back, making space for me, I crouch down to look at the bloodstains spread across Dominguez's shirt.

"I don't think he turned," I say quietly.

"Ma'am?"

I point at the tight cluster of entry wounds. "There

are our four gunshots," I say. "Grouping is tight, isolated to center of mass. If Dominguez had started to turn around as he was hit, that group would've shifted either right or left, depending on how he moved. But the entry wounds are all in a bunch, no trailing. Whoever shot him did it quickly, efficiently."

I pull my notebook and pen out to scribble a quick note to myself about the detail and to follow up with the medical examiner later.

"Thank you," I tell the tech before standing. "If you find anything interesting, let me or Detective Cross know." She goes back to processing the scene, and I head to the back of the house before turning to face the front entry.

I drop into Second-Sight and take in the body. Outlined in bright, shimmering light, it's almost like life has come back into the corpse. It shifts and shivers, but it's not the same movement as breath, as life. I drink in the rest of the scene, searching for any hint of the red-black energy. Thankfully, there's no immediate sign of it. Trying to sense it lingering or hiding somewhere, insidious and invisible, I push farther, spreading my power out in a thin veil around the house, but find nothing. It's a small relief, all things considered, and I appreciate it. As I fall out of Second-Sight, I take in the spatter of blood on the walls and floor, bringing myself back to the more pressing, immediate problem at hand.

You think I can get a Reading off of blood? I ask Priya with a shiver.

She appears next to me and frowns at the gore

around us. *Maybe. I haven't heard of people doing that before.*

Me neither. I sigh. *I'd also rather not. I haven't exactly had the best of luck with it in the past.*

That's a delicate way of saying it's gone to hell every time.

I frown at her. *Do you think he's been living here long?*

No idea. You're the cop.

I don't see a lot of personal items in the house. No pictures on the walls, no books or random things lying around. Maybe he moved in recently. Shaking my head, I look toward the rear entrance and back at the front door. *So, the attacker breaks the glass, unlocks the door, then comes through the house. Dominguez has his back to them. They fire four times, Dominguez goes down, and they leave. In and out, quick and clean.*

So why doesn't Dominguez turn around when the glass breaks? Priya asks. *The guy's narking on the Latin Kings. I'd think he would be paranoid about being found out. If I were in his shoes and heard glass breaking, I'd be making a break for it.*

Maybe he was running from the back of the house toward the front door when he got shot.

And he doesn't look back to see what's happening? Just takes off running immediately? She shakes her head. *Even if he was expecting it, it's human nature to look toward loud sounds. He might've started running right* after *looking, but he would've turned at least a little bit.* Priya points to the body on the floor. *And look at how he's lying on the floor. If he had been running when he was shot, he'd be more forward than he is, right? Sprawled out? The momentum would've carried his body forward, and his arm probably wouldn't have gotten trapped underneath him, not like that.*

I look again and notice she's right. Dominguez's right arm is pinned under his chest, the tips of his fingers barely visible where his neck meets his left shoulder. If he'd been running before being shot, he would've fallen forward, his arms stretching out to catch himself as he fell, less likely to get caught under his body.

And, she continues, *the blood drops would've had tails if he was running.*

The pool of blood around Dominguez's body makes it hard to see any blood droplets, but when I kneel, I see that Priya is right. There are blood drops on the floor, but they're circular, rather than ovoid. They fell straight down, not from someone moving.

Well, fuck, I say. Confused, I turn back to look at the broken glass in the back door. *Why didn't he turn around?*

Chapter Three

I walk to the kitchen and Cross comes into view. He's looking at the broken glass on the floor, frowning.

"Hey," I say as I stop next to him. "We've got a problem."

"Another one?" He raises a brow.

"Yeah." I point back to our victim. "I can't figure this out, and I need you to help me go ove—"

"Detectives," a tech says excitedly. "We've got blood on the door."

Cross and I both turn. Crouching next to the broken pane, the tech is pointing at a jagged piece of glass still stuck in the doorframe. As he moves a penlight over the surface, light refracts through the broken planes and red blooms. It's not a lot of blood, but it clings to the edge, standing out now that the tech's drawn our attention to it.

"You think our killer cut themselves when they busted in the glass?" Cross asks.

"Looks like. Any sign of prints?" The tech is carefully collecting the blood when I ask.

He shakes his head. "No, ma'am. We haven't found anything yet."

"So, our perp is careful enough to not leave prints but doesn't notice that he was cut badly enough to leave blood at the scene?" I ask.

"He might not have been paying attention when it happened," Cross answers. "Too keyed up on adrenaline."

"Maybe," I say, still unconvinced.

"We're missing a trail through the glass back here, too," Cross says. "It could be that more fell from the pane when the attacker left, and it's disguising where he walked through the crime scene, but it doesn't look right."

Something is off with the scene, but I can't put my finger on it. I motion to Cross. "Follow me."

I lead him to the front of the house and explain what Priya and I discussed. He listens attentively, nodding along as I speak, but he's frowning with me by the end.

"You think Priya could pass the detective's exam at this point?" he asks. His eyes go distant, and I hear Priya laugh.

He's very complimentary, she tells me with a wide grin, her cheeks darkened by a blush. *I do like the man.*

Hands off. I let a thread of amused affection trickle down our bond. *I called dibs.*

She sighs. *Fine. Be that way.*

"Let's run through this," Cross says, turning his attention back to me. "Dominguez is inside. The attacker breaks the back window, unlocks the door, and comes into the house."

"So, why doesn't he turn?" I ask again.

"TV's on. Dominguez mistakes the noise for something happening on screen?"

"Except the television was off when we arrived."

"So were the lights, but they came on. The TV could be on a timer, too."

"Okay, good point," I say with a conciliatory nod.

"Alternatively," Cross continues, "the attacker could have been here before Dominguez was. He lies in wait, then attacks when Dominguez's back is turned."

"And Dominguez doesn't notice the broken glass?"

Cross gives me an irritated look. "Just throwing ideas out here, Phillips."

"All right, don't get huffy." I look around the small house, taking in the lack of hiding places. I head toward one of the two bedrooms and stand inside the doorway. "You be Dominguez, I'll be the killer."

Cross nods and stands near the front entry, his back to me.

"So, I approach from behind, gun drawn." I count off the shots. "You're down on the floor before you even see me."

"We're going to have to get the medical examiner to confirm the angle of entry on those gunshots," Cross says with a shake of his head. "I couldn't see you approaching, but if the attack came from the back instead of the side, I wouldn't be able to see the killer approaching, either."

I shrug. "Either way, Dominguez is dead. I pick up my casings, wipe down everything I touched—"

Cross interrupts. "Or you're wearing gloves."

"Or I'm wearing gloves," I agree, "and then I leave through the back."

We walk to the back door, and I step carefully around the scattered glass shards. The glass isn't tempered, so there are large, jagged pieces lying on the floor, some broken in half from hitting the ground. As I crouch down for a closer look, Cross joins me.

"Do you see what I mean about the trail?" he asks.

Up close, I do. If someone had walked on any of the large pieces of glass on the floor, the point where the person's foot came into contact with the glass would be shattered, with cracks and lines radiating out from that point. Instead, most of the glass on the ground is comparably intact, just large, triangular pieces that fell from the door.

"Could he have walked around them?" I ask. "We've been doing that."

Cross frowns. "Why would he, though? What's he gain from not stepping on the glass? He's already made noise entering the residence."

"Something isn't right here." I shake my head. "What are we missing?"

Cross and I look at each other, uncertainty coursing through me. It's not a feeling I'm used to and I can't say I like it.

"Let's focus on what we can figure out for now," Cross offers. He turns to the tech. "Get a sample of the glass from the door and the floor. I want to know as much about how this stuff broke as possible."

"Yes, Detective," he says and returns to his work.

"You want to wait for the medical examiner to get here?" Cross asks.

I shake my head. "The most important information we need from the body is how those bullets entered and we're not going to get that until the autopsy."

"That's going to take some time," Cross says.

"Hopefully, we'll have a preliminary report before the end of the day. In the meantime, we can look into Dominguez's known associates. You want to drive?"

Cross shrugs but takes the keys for the surveillance vehicle when I offer them.

We're, thankfully, not far from District HQ. It's still early enough that the roads aren't busy, but it picks up as we drive, commuters heading out to their various jobs and the night shift heading home. I watch as cars drift past us. My eyelids are heavy, and with the gentle shift of the car and the hum of the road beneath us, I don't notice when I doze off.

I wake up when Cross gently shakes my shoulder. He smiles at me, eyes soft and full of amusement.

"Hey, sleepyhead."

"Shut up," I say, though it's ruined when I can't hold back a yawn.

He laughs, then climbs out of the car. "Let's see

what we can learn about our victim." He leans into the car, arms draped over the door and the roof. "And get you some coffee. You never got your hands on some at the scene."

My car door slams loudly in the parking lot, and I trail after him, blinking sleep from my eyes. "How are you this awake?" I mutter, though it's lacking any venom.

"I found a caffeine pill in the glove compartment while you were asleep."

I glare at his back and fight the urge to sigh. "You're the worst."

He holds the front door open for me, his grin barely held in check.

The bull pen is crowded, even though it's still early. Uniformed officers walk around with folders of paperwork. Other detectives are hunched over their desks or quietly discussing cases as they sip coffee from CPD mugs. A few of them wave at Cross and me as we head toward our back corner. I return the gesture, though I'm more interested in caffeine than stopping for small talk.

Cross shrugs out of his jacket and lays it carefully over the back of his chair while I keep walking toward the kitchen. The coffee maker is full, and I pour two cups before heading back to our desks.

After setting Cross's cup in front of him, I take a careful sip of coffee. It's almost too hot, the liquid a little shy of scalding. I drink it greedily. I'll crash if I don't do something to combat the exhaustion soon, and the sting of pain helps wake me up.

With a sigh, I plop into my desk chair. It screeches in protest, and eyes turn toward us, then roll away.

"So," I ask after taking another, smaller, sip. "What do we have on this guy?"

Cross finishes booting up his computer and starts to type. It takes a few moments for his computer to spit back the results, but when it does, he raises his eyebrows.

"Well…" He sounds hesitant. "We're not going to have a problem finding people Dominguez knew."

"How many known associates are we looking at?"

"I've got ten to fifteen names on the list in the system." He scrolls, then frowns. "Okay, make that twenty. This guy got around."

"All gang related?"

"Looks like it, yes. We've got gun runners, drug dealers, one assault with a deadly weapon…"

I whistle. "Our boy was a regular social butterfly."

"Seems so." He leans back, and a printer whirs to life nearby. "I'm printing a list. It might not hurt to go over it with Martinez, see if we can rule some of these people out."

"Good idea. I'll give him a call."

Cross nods. He leans forward, skimming through the search results, his forehead wrinkling in concentration. I roll my eyes, amused, and grab my desk phone to dial Martinez's number.

"Detective Carlos Martinez," he says, voice sharp.

"It's Phillips. Cross and I were hoping we could have a few minutes of your time to go over the list of known associates we pulled for Dominguez."

Martinez sighs. "Yeah, I can do that, but I won't be free for another hour or two. I'm tied up right now."

"Anything we need to know about?"

"No, not yet. For now, focus on the criminal side of things."

"Gotcha. When you get free, meet us at District Seven HQ, and we'll grab a conference room."

"Sounds good." He pauses. "You find anything on scene?"

"Not much, no. A couple of things that don't fit perfectly, but it should make more sense once we get the autopsy report. Forensics did find a blood sample, though. Probably the killer's."

He lets out a slow breath. "Fantastic. I know it'll take some time for them to run it, but if you get any hits, let me know." Someone yells in the background, their voice too indistinct for me to make out the words. "Yeah, I'm coming!" Martinez yells back. "I'll call you when I'm on my way."

"See you then," I say before hanging up.

Cross sets a list of names in front of me.

"You start at the top, I'll go from the bottom?" I suggest.

He grins. "Meet you in the middle, then."

Looking through criminal records is far from glamorous, but it's a big part of the job. I'm able to rule out the first name—James "Jimmy" Anderson—almost immediately, as he's been locked up in the Cook County Jail for the last six months. The next name on the list, a Cisco Rivera, is out on bail for a drug charge. I note his home address and number, then move onto Dwayne Turner. He's been clean for a while, no new arrests on his record for the last year and a half. It's good news since he might be willing to turn on one of his old associates if he's gone straight. I'm about to enter the next name on the list—Nathan Herrera—when I hear my name echoing across the bull pen.

"Phillips! Cross!"

I whip my head up to find Lieutenant Walker leaning out of her office, her expression stormy.

That can't be good.

"Get your asses in here!"

I glance at Cross. He looks as confused as I feel, but he jumps to his feet and hurries toward Walker's office. I speed after him, avoiding the amused glances of the other officers in the bull pen. I don't like to think I've earned a reputation for getting in trouble with the brass, but if it quacks like a duck…

When I enter her office, Walker is leaning against her desk, arms crossed as she glares at Cross and me.

"Shut the door."

Definitely not good.

I close it carefully and make my way to a seat. Walker looks at me, waiting until I sit to start talking.

"Want to explain to me how you managed to get a

murder out of a surveillance op?"

"Uh…" I trail off and look to Cross for help.

"We believe the suspect may have been dead when we started our shift, ma'am," he says.

Walker pinches the bridge of her nose. "And you didn't confirm that the suspect was inside and *alive* when you started said shift?"

"The officers we were replacing verified that they'd seen the suspect enter the building and not exit. We didn't have any reason to believe that he wasn't having a quiet night at home."

She sighs. "So, he was killed while Chicago police were parked right outside his house. Shot *four times* without *anyone* hearing anything?" She slams her hand down on the table. "That's bullshit. Goddamnit."

As she stalks to the chair behind her desk, my heart races. I haven't seen Walker this pissed in a long time. When she sits down heavily in her chair, leaning back to stare at the ceiling, I tense.

"There's going to be hell to pay—I hope you understand that. And don't think you're the only ones who are going to catch crap for this." She looks back at us. "Martinez already told me you're in the know about Dominguez."

When we nod, she continues. "I don't think you understand the magnitude of what's going on here. I'm not at liberty to fill you in on all the details, but there're a lot of moving parts that got fucked to hell and back because this guy is dead. We've got a rat, and he's trying to shut up anyone who might know who he is."

She leans forward. "You two? You're going to figure out who killed this CI, you got me? Use whatever resources you need, but you find this asshole as soon as possible. This is your highest priority."

"Yes, ma'am," I say.

"And you," she says, pointing at me. "Use your"—she wiggles her fingers—"Medium shit while working this. I'll get the authorization paperwork started, but I don't want us missing anything while it's fresh. You need to draw your little circles or use blood or whatever voodoo you do? Do it. You need to pull in more Mediums? Done. I want this guy found and locked up, and I want it done fast."

I nod, and she waves us away. "Get back to work. I've got a fucking mess to clean up."

Chapter Four

Cross and I put our heads down after that, digging through the list of names and finding contact information whenever possible. By the end of it, we've winnowed the list down from twenty-two names to eleven. It's still a huge number of people to interview. Even if they weren't all career criminals with rap sheets longer than my arm, it would be a major undertaking. Since these guys are going to be more than a little unhappy to talk to the police, it only makes the situation worse.

"So, we start with Herrera and move on to Turner and Smith," Cross is saying when my phone rings. He stops speaking as I answer.

"Detective Phillips."

"Hey, it's Martinez. You guys free?"

"Yeah," I say, mouthing Martinez's name to Cross. "We're working on the known acquaintances right now. How far out are you?"

"Should be there in ten to fifteen."

"Perfect. We'll have a cup of coffee waiting."

I hang up and lean back in my chair. "Guess we can

hold off on figuring out who to interview for a bit."

"Fantastic," Cross says as he tosses the list onto his desk. "This is going to suck."

"Yup." I pop the P, then sigh. "We'll get through it, though. At least we're not juggling other cases at the same time."

Cross leans forward, his elbows resting on his desk as he lowers his voice. "Whatever this op is, it's got to be big. Walker wouldn't pull us off our other cases if this weren't something major."

"You think we can get anything out of Martinez?"

"Maybe." He doesn't sound convinced. "It'll probably depend on IA. If we're running a criminal case in parallel to theirs…"

"They won't want to contaminate whatever work we're doing." I nod. "Yeah, that was my thought, too."

"But maybe," he says, giving me a pointed look, "if you can charm him…"

My eyebrows raise. "What are you talking about?"

"He likes you," Cross continues. "He caved to your particular brand of charisma earlier. Might as well try your luck a second time."

"Martinez does not like me." I shake my head. "You've known him as long as I have, and he's never once had a nice thing to say about me."

Cross waves off my comment. "That's because you intimidate him. Trust me, he likes you."

"I think you're projecting."

"Oh, I know I am." He grins. "You definitely

intimidate me."

Laughing, I turn back to my screen. "Whatever. You're friends with him. That'll get us farther than anything I have to say."

"You seriously underestimate yourself, Kim," he says with sincerity. "You've got a way with people, even when you're prickly."

"Prickly."

He rolls his eyes. "You know what I mean."

I do, unfortunately.

"Fine," I huff. "I'll try it your way, and when I prove you wrong, you can buy me dinner."

"Deal." His eyes twinkle. "Though I would've bought you dinner anyway."

"Whatever you say." I grab his coffee cup along with mine and walk to the kitchen for a refill.

A few minutes later, Martinez walks into district HQ and heads straight for our desks. He glances around the bull pen. If I weren't looking for it, I would've missed the wary glint in his eyes. My gut tightens. Whatever he knows, it's got him looking at the other officers in our district with distrust.

Cross and I stand as Martinez approaches our desks.

"Afternoon, Detectives," he says as he shrugs out of his coat. "You got that coffee for me?"

I pass him the disposable cup I grabbed when I refilled our cups earlier. "Conference Room A is open." I nod my head toward it and let Cross lead the way.

Martinez is between us, and it feels like we're taking

a suspect in for an interrogation rather than going to talk with a fellow officer. The hairs on the back of my neck stand up, and when I glance behind me, wary eyes are watching us, though they dart away as I look. Nerves dance through me, and I shrug them aside as we walk into the conference room. I close the door between us and the rest of the bull pen and wait for Martinez to take a seat.

He almost falls into a chair, his shoulders sagging as he fiddles with his coffee cup. He doesn't drink, only looks at it as if it holds answers to the questions he doesn't know how to ask.

"So," he says at last on a slow exhale, "what do you want to know?" When Cross and I exchange a glance, Martinez rolls his eyes. "Your lieutenant vouched for you and cleared it with my captain. I'm a… fairly open book."

"What the fuck is going on?" I ask, and Cross coughs to cover his surprised laugh.

"Sit," Martinez says, shooting Cross a quelling look. "It's… complicated."

"No shit."

Martinez turns his glare on me, then waits for Cross to take a seat. "We got an anonymous tip about seven, eight months back that someone in the CPD was working with the Latin Kings. The tipster didn't name anyone, but they gave us intel about some evidence that had gone missing."

"Did Evidence know that it was missing?" Cross asks.

Martinez shakes his head. "No, they had no idea that anything had disappeared from storage. If the tipster hadn't told us about it, it would've been months before anyone noticed, if not longer."

"I know we're supposed to keep everything almost indefinitely, but evidence does go missing," Cross continues. "Especially with older cases."

I lean forward. "What are we talking about here? Why did *this* evidence matter?"

"You remember that drive-by, where the kid got caught in the crossfire?" Martinez asks.

I wince. "Vividly."

It had dominated the news for months. A seven-year-old boy, walking home from school, was in the wrong place at the wrong time. His mother had sobbed her way through interview after interview, asking for someone, *anyone*, to speak up about the shooters.

The silence from the community and the CPD had been deafening.

"We had CCTV footage of the car. It was grainy but good enough to make out part of the driver's face. Forensics had already been through it, but the original tape and the stills they took are gone. As far as we can tell, someone walked into Evidence, took the originals, wiped the digital copies, and walked out."

"Well, shit." Cross breathes out heavily. "And there's no record of an officer accessing the system?"

Martinez shakes his head. "No. They used a generic login that the IT guys have for admin access, and before you ask, no, they don't know how our perp got the password for it."

"And somehow, the Latin Kings are involved?" Cross asks.

"That's what the tipster said. The victim—the *intended* victim—was on their bad side. It had been a planned hit as far as Organized Crime was able to figure out."

"So, it was only about this drive-by?" I frown. "Why would an officer want to help them cover that up? What does a police officer gain from protecting a child killer?"

Martinez shakes his head. "It's more than that. The tipster was able to tell us about missing money, drugs, important physical evidence. Again, no records indicating who ran off with all of it and nothing on tape. We don't even know if it's one cop or many who are involved in this."

Cross sighs. "Let me guess. Dominguez was your tipster."

"Yeah. That dead kid…" Martinez trails off, shaking his head. "It bothered Dominguez. He's got a little brother around that age, took the death personally. But he was afraid. Of the Kings, of the cops, of everyone."

"At the crime scene," I say, "you told us that Dominguez had told you about ops that went sideways, not about missing evidence."

Martinez nods. "He started coming to us more after his initial report. I didn't ask him why, figured I wouldn't push my luck, but I think he felt like he was doing something good for his community. Helping people." He shrugs. "Whatever the reason, he was a solid CI."

"When did he tell you about the dirty cop?"

"He first mentioned it about three months ago. Dominguez kept it vague to start with, but once we realized what he was hinting at, we… *I* started pushing for him to give us more intel."

Cross frowns. "But he didn't."

"Oh, he gave us plenty of intel. I wanted a *name*. I hounded him about it. But he wanted into witness protection," Martinez explains. "Until then, he didn't feel safe telling us who was involved."

"So, why were we surveilling him?" I ask. "It sounds like he was cooperating, at least partially."

"I wanted him safeguarded." Martinez shakes his head. "It was meant to be a temporary thing, a stopgap while I waited for the witness protection paperwork to process. I made sure he moved around, didn't stay in one place for too long."

"You used surveillance teams to monitor him, to make sure he wasn't alone," Cross says. "So, the Kings—or the cops—couldn't get to him."

"Exactly."

"Doesn't seem to have worked out for you," I mutter.

He glares at me.

"What Phillips meant to say is—" Cross starts, but I hold a hand up.

"I said what I meant." I look pointedly at Martinez.

"What're the next steps here? Your CI is dead, you don't have any leads, and now we've got a murder to solve, plus a PR nightmare."

"I didn't say I didn't have *any* leads." Martinez glares at me. "We've been able to narrow down a list of possible officers. It's not long, but they all have some kind of connection with the cases where evidence went missing and have been working in the Latin Kings's territory for more than five years. It's not much, but it's what we've got."

"You going to give us the list?"

Martinez flips me off. "No, and you already know that."

"Fine." I lean back in my chair and cross my arms. "But you know it's only going to slow us down."

"It's only going to stop you from being unduly influenced by an IA investigation."

"He has a point, Kim," Cross says, though he looks irritated. "We can't go into this with a suspect already in mind."

"Do you have any other CIs who could help us out here? Anyone willing to speak up or point fingers?"

"No." Martinez deflates. "We've got other CIs, but none of them are members of the Latin Kings. The gang is notoriously tight-lipped, and that's not changing with Dominguez dead."

"So, we work the evidence." I sigh. "You'd better hope this guy fucked up and left something behind."

"Other than a blood sample?"

"You going to get DNA from all those cops on your list? You and I both know that police don't want to give up DNA if the courts aren't mandating it."

"Can you blame them?" Martinez asks. After a moment, he runs his fingers through his hair and sighs. "If we have to get a warrant for it, we can go that route. In the meantime, I need you two to do what you're good at, which is solving murders with fuck-all for evidence. I mean, c'mon. You found Jackie Harris. At least this one is fresh."

Cross sighs. "Okay. If you get to the point where you can tell us anything, you've got our numbers. In the meantime"—he passes our list of known associates to Martinez—"if you can cross any of these assholes off our list, we'd appreciate it."

Martinez frowns down at the paper, then pulls a pen from his jacket before crossing off three names. "I'm pretty sure these guys aren't involved in the downtown racket. They work in the area but tend to be out in the suburbs, mainly Elgin." He pushes the list back to us. "That's it, though."

Eight names. Eight career criminals spread out across the South Side of Chicago. I groan internally but try to keep my disappointment from my face. Standing, I gesture toward the door. "Thank you for coming by, Martinez."

He gets to his feet. "Of course. Call me if you find anything."

Martinez stands there awkwardly as Cross stays seated. I open the door for him and wait for him to leave. Hands tucked into his pockets, he nods at me, then walks out. Shutting the door behind him, I turn to Cross.

"Charming enough?" I smirk.

"You can't tell by the stars in my eyes?" he says, deadpan. "What do you want to do about this?"

I sit and lean forward, my arms on the table, hands clasped. "We could try to figure out who's on Martinez's list."

"We'd only be able to look at officers who've been working in Latin Kings territory, and that's probably more than half of the CPD. Without knowing which cases had evidence go missing, we won't be able to narrow the field, and, if I had to guess, Martinez or IA or *both* have already cleaned up that paper trail to stop anyone else from doing exactly that."

I frown, hating that he's probably right. "Then, I guess we've got eight guys with massive criminal records to go find and talk to."

"Don't sound so excited, Phillips," Cross says. "If you ask nicely, I'll even let you drive."

CHAPTER FIVE

We find Herrera hanging out on a corner near Wentworth and 72nd Street. He's leaning against the wall of a bodega, the bright advertisements next to him in stark contrast to his dark demeanor. He's wearing dirty jeans with a rip in the knee, a long white T-shirt with black text in a thick calligraphic font stretched across the front, and a yellow quilted jacket that he's left open. Hands tucked into his jeans, his eyes are dark and shadowed, his brow hidden beneath a black knit cap. When Cross and I approach, he shifts his weight and grins.

"Nathan Herrera?" I ask.

He gives me a slow once-over. "What d'you want, *mami*?"

I flash him my badge, and his grin widens. "We'd like to talk to you."

"I don't talk to cops," he says, pushing off the wall. He walks between Cross and me, giving me another sidelong glance as he moves past. "Not even sexy ones."

I grimace. "How about murder cops?"

"Hey, I don't get involved in that shit." He peers

over his shoulder at us. This time, his look is cautious, considering. The lecherous, insolent expression is gone.

All that remains is uncertainty and distrust.

"You know a guy named Dominguez?" Cross asks.

Herrera spits. "I don't speak ill of the dead, but fuck that guy."

"You know what happened to him, then?"

"Yeah." Herrera lifts his chin, sneering. "He got what was coming to him."

"And what was that?"

"A bullet."

"So, maybe you *do* get involved in this shit," I say.

Herrera laughs. "Word moves fast, *mami*. Don't have to be involved to know that. Especially when there were pigs sitting right outside when it happened. Serve and protect, my ass."

Cross doesn't say anything, only tenses his jaw, but something in his eyes makes Herrera nervous. The kid takes a hesitant step away from us.

"Anyway, I didn't have anything to do with that. I knew the guy, but that's it."

"You want to tell us how you knew him?" I press, hoping he'll give us something useful.

He shrugs. "From the neighborhood. Saw him around, you know. We weren't friends or anything."

"Your record says you were close enough to deal together."

He scoffs. "You don't have to be close to someone to get picked up with them. Wrong time, wrong place.

That was it. I wasn't even carrying."

"So, it didn't have anything to do with your gang affiliations? I'd think that would've made you brothers," Cross says.

"I don't talk about that shit." Herrera glares in defiance, then turns his attention to me, pretending like Cross isn't there. "You gonna arrest me, or you just waiting for me to give you my number? I won't fight if you wanna cuff me, *mami*."

Part of me wants to laugh at how blatant the kid is being, but I roll my eyes instead. "We want to talk to you."

"We've talked. You need anything else?" He winks at me.

"No," Cross answers through clenched teeth. "But we'll be around."

"Yeah." Herrera gives Cross a hard look. "Sure, you will."

I can sense Cross's tension growing as the kid walks away. When he turns the corner, disappearing from sight, Cross curses low under his breath and spins around, walking back toward our car.

How old is that guy? Priya asks.

His file says he's twenty-two.

She lets out a long sigh. *He makes me feel ancient.*

By the time I catch up, Cross is climbing into the cruiser. I wrench my door open and hurry inside. As I close it, though, I notice that Cross hasn't started the car. Instead, he's sitting with both hands on the steering wheel, eyes trained on the dashboard, knuckles white.

"You okay?" I ask hesitantly, not understanding the mood that's darkened his expression.

"Yeah," he says, shaken out of his stupor by my voice. "I'm just irritated."

"About what?" I ask, still confused.

He jams the key into the ignition and turns the car on. "The shit he was saying about police."

"He's only a kid," I say. "He's grown up in and around gangs, and we're cops. He's going to be an asshole about that."

"It doesn't help that we look like idiots."

Understanding dawns. "Is this about him calling us out for being in front of the house when Dominguez was killed?"

Judging by the flush that suffuses his cheeks, it is.

"Riley," I say, setting my hand on his arm. "We didn't hear anything, and as far as we knew, Dominguez was asleep. Yeah, it sucks that we weren't able to stop a murder, but for all we know, it happened before we were parked out front. You shouldn't beat yourself up about it."

"But we failed him," Cross says, his voice heavy with anger and disappointment. "That kid put his life at risk to inform on some bad people. We were supposed to protect him and we didn't."

"He knew what the risks were," I say. "He knew what coming to the police would mean, the danger it would put him in. From what Martinez told us, he was still willing to talk."

He sighs. "You're right. But I don't like that Herrera guy."

"And you think I do?" I scoff. "He's a kid who's made bad decisions, been forced to make bad decisions, and now he's living with the repercussions. And"—I lean back in my seat in a defeated slump—"he's a bust as a character witness. There's no way he's going to talk to us about Dominguez."

"Not even if hell froze over," Cross agrees. "Fuck, how are we going to find out anything about this guy?"

"We keep going down the list and hope someone is willing to talk," I say, though I don't sound optimistic. "Who's next?"

"Cisco Rivera," Cross says. "Couple drug charges, nothing violent. We're not far from his work address."

A few minutes later, we pull up to a partially empty strip mall. There are a few storefronts with leasing signs in the windows, the large fonts faded by sun and time. The stores that are occupied are a mixed bag. There's a Salvation Army, a flower shop, and a dollar store. The place we're interested in, though, is at the end of the strip.

Rivera Dry Cleaning is painted on the front window in wide, white letters, and through the glass, I see an older Hispanic woman standing behind a low counter. Her dark hair is threaded through with white and tossed up into a messy bun. Her shirt is black, and she's wearing a white apron on top of it, the upper half folded over and tied around her waist instead of around her neck. She looks up and, when she does, catches sight of our car and our watchful eyes. Slowly, she pales and places a trembling hand on the counter. Though I can tell she's bracing herself for bad news, I don't see weakness in the set of her shoulders or her rigid posture.

She looks like she's getting ready for war.

"One down, seven more to go," I say, already exhausted, before getting out of the car.

A bell above the door rings cheerfully as Cross and I enter the dry cleaners. The woman, who's come out from around the counter, has her arms crossed though her expression is stoic, any hint of the emotions from earlier hidden away.

"How can I help you, officers?" Her voice is low and slightly rough, and her Hispanic accent is light.

"We're looking for Cisco Rivera," Cross says. "This is listed as his place of employment."

"It is." Her words are clipped.

"May I ask your name, ma'am?" He smiles, but she's unmoved by his kind expression.

"Mrs. Rivera," she says.

Her polite hostility makes sense now.

"Cisco is your husband?" I guess.

"*Francisco* is my son. What's he done this time? Is it drugs again?"

"No, ma'am," Cross says, trying his smile again. Her expression softens. "We were hoping to speak to him about a friend of his. Do you happen to know where your son is?"

"No." Her hands tangle in her apron and the wrinkles near her eyes deepen. "I haven't seen him for a few days. I thought that he'd been picked up by the police again. After last time, I told him to not call me to bail him out."

"Do you know how we could find him?" Cross presses.

The woman bites her lip. "I don't think he'd like me talking to the police."

"Ma'am," I say gently, "we're not with Narcotics. We're with Homicide."

Her face goes white. "Is he okay? What did he do?"

"He's fine, and he's not in trouble with us," I say, trying to calm her. "Someone who your son knows was killed. We were hoping Francisco would be able to help us."

She curses quietly in Spanish. "I told him not to get messed up in all of this. Who was it?"

"A young man named Juan Dominguez." Cross pulls a photograph from his pocket of the victim and hands it to Mrs. Rivera. "According to our records, they knew each other."

She gives the picture a long, considering look but shakes her head before handing it back to Cross.

"I haven't seen him around here in a while. He and Francisco grew up together. They got into a lot of trouble as boys." A wry smile peeks out but disappears just as quickly. "Before the gang stuff, I mean. Once Francisco got out of high school…"

"Can you tell us where and when you last saw either Juan or your son?"

"Like I said, I saw Francisco a few days ago, maybe four? He lives with me and got home late from his second job. I heard him come in, then go to his room. I checked in on him before I left to open the store."

"And Juan?"

She bites at her lip as she thinks. "Maybe two months ago? He stopped hanging around the neighborhood. I think he moved, maybe?"

"You have any idea where?" Cross asks. "Doesn't have to be specific, but if you could point us in the right direction."

"No, I'm sorry. I don't know anything more than that. You'd have to talk to my son."

"Can you give us the address of his second job?"

She nods and grabs a book of dry cleaning tickets and a pen. After tearing one from the pad, she writes on the blank back and hands it to me.

"It's not far," she adds, her hands tangling together now that they're empty. "But I called, and they haven't seen him either."

"We'll follow up with them just in case." I pull a business card from my jacket pocket. "Please, take this." I pass it to her. "If you hear from your son, can you have him give us a call?"

She puts my business card in her apron pocket. "I'll tell him to call, though I don't know if he will."

"We'd appreciate any additional help he can provide.

Thank you for your time, ma'am," Cross says and heads toward the door, holding it open for me. I duck past him and start walking toward the car.

As soon as Cross closes his door, I curse. "This is going to end up being a waste of time, isn't it?"

He sighs. "We still have six other people to talk to, and Rivera's second job to follow up with. Someone is going to know something useful."

"But we both know they probably won't say anything to us." I groan and put my head in my hands. "We've got to be able to do something to speed this up. Maybe I should get my own car? We'll get through this list faster if we split up."

Cross frowns. "That's an option, but I don't like it. We work well together, and I don't see how saving a couple of hours tracking these guys down is going to make a difference in this case."

"Walker wants it done fast. If we're together, hunting down the same guy, we're going to lose time."

Do we know how long Dominguez was living in that house? Priya asks, interrupting before Cross can say anything else.

I frown, thrown off by her question. *No, I didn't think to check.*

"Why would that matter?" Cross asks as he starts the car.

The longer someone lives somewhere, the more emotional energy they invest in the place.

At Cross's and my blank expressions, she rolls her

eyes.

Which means it's easier to Read.

Cross looks surprised. "You think Kim could Read something in the house?"

"If he's got some personal possessions there, it's possible," I say cautiously. "But only if he put some kind of emotional investment into it. His toothbrush, for example, would be useless."

You should call Martinez. He'd know how long Dominguez was there since he was in charge of relocating him.

"You want to try and find the next guy on the list first?" He looks down and groans. "Frank Brown. Fantastic. I bet he'll be really easy to track down."

I dig for my phone. "Let's see what Martinez has to say."

The other detective's phone rings over to voice mail, so I hang up and try again. I'm counting the rings, certain the line's going to click over again when he picks up.

"What do you want, Phillips? Aren't you working a homicide?"

"And hello to you, too, darling," I say coyly. "I've missed our loving conversations."

"Can you cut the bullshit, please? We've both got a fuckton of work to do."

"That's why I'm calling, actually," I say as I look at Cross. "How long was Dominguez holed up in the house where he was killed?"

"Not long," Martinez says, and I curse internally. "I

made sure he moved from place to place pretty frequently. Didn't want someone to find him, you know?"

"Any chance you can be more specific on the timeline?"

I can hear Martinez's eye roll. "I dunno, five days? Maybe six?"

"Not any longer?"

"No," he says, sounding annoyed.

"Thank you." I try my best to sound sincerely grateful, though I want to grit my teeth. "Cross and I may be heading back to the scene. I want to try something."

Silence, then, "I don't like the sound of that."

"I got the okay from Walker already," I hedge. "It'll be fine."

"Please," Martinez says, sounding pained, "*please* don't fuck up my crime scene."

"It's *my* crime scene and it'll be fine. We'll talk later. Tell the kids I love them, okay?"

Martinez's irritated voice spills out from the speaker for a second before I hang up.

"I'm glad you didn't go into medicine," Cross says as he starts the cruiser. "I can't imagine what your bedside manner would've been like."

Honestly, Priya says, *that was restrained for her. She's gotten a lot better since she started working with you.*

"I haven't had to beat up a suspect or threaten a witness in months," I say in a falsely cheerful voice and glare at Cross and Priya. "Can we go?"

CHAPTER SIX

In the light of day, the house where Dominguez was killed looks barren and broken down. The siding is peeling on one side, and there are splotches of newer paint across the front of the home where it's been repaired. The concrete steps leading up to the front door are cracked and wobble as Cross and I climb them.

"Do you seriously think this is going to work?" he asks, frowning as I cut through the crime scene seal on the door. He passes me a pair of gloves and shoe covers and I slide them on.

"I'm hoping that our victim really liked this place," I answer as I push my way inside. "If I can Read something in here, we might be able to piece together some of this mess. Hopefully, there's a memory or two hiding in here."

Our footsteps crinkle as we walk inside, both of us careful to avoid the dark bloodstain spread across the front entryway. Cross walks through the living room and into the kitchen while I detour to the first bedroom.

The mattress on the floor has seen much better days. The sheets covering it are dingy, though they don't look dirty. A laundry basket piled high with men's clothing is tucked into the corner, and as I pick a shirt up from it and give it a sniff, I frown. They're also clean, though apparently someone didn't care about folding and putting their stuff away.

A stranger after my own heart.

In the corner of the room, there's a closet that's barely big enough to deserve the name. The door is hanging open, so I reach in and pull the cord to turn on the bare bulb inside. It flickers as I peer into the storage space. There are worn shoes on the floor, as well as a cardboard box with GOODWILL written across the top in thick, black lines. When I pull it open, I find more clothes, though these are worn and threadbare.

I dig through the contents, pulling out the most worn pieces I can find. There's a black-and-yellow plaid shirt, and though the yellow is more mustard than gold, I take it as a good sign. It's Latin Kings colors, which means it may have meant something to a guy who'd been part of the gang for a while and turned on them. Setting it aside, I also pull out a faded graphic tee with a large hole along the side seam and a pair of jeans with a faded outline of a phone on the back pocket, both evidently favorites of whoever owned them. I'm about to stand when instinct has me grabbing the shoes, too. My arms are a little overfull, which leaves me juggling the clothing a bit, but I get it gathered together and leave.

When I walk back into the living room, my arms full of clothes, Cross gives me a confused look.

"They're worn," I say. "Well-used."

"Invested in, emotionally?" he hedges.

"That's the hope."

He frowns as I set the clothes down on the kitchen table and bend to pull my knife from my boot. The silver glints in the half-light streaming through the broken back door window, and as I remove my gloves, Cross takes a hesitant step forward.

"Don't you have to use blood for a Reading?" he asks.

"That seems to be the running theme, yes."

"You're going to contaminate the crime scene."

I glare at him. "Then it's a good thing Forensics has been through here already."

With a wince, I pierce the skin on my finger and watch as the blood wells up. I wait until it forms a perfect, ruby red drop, then press my finger against the black-and-yellow shirt.

It doesn't have the same feel as Comfort's diary or Alvarez's notebook. There's no memory deeply inlaid in the fabric of the shirt, no thread of emotion woven into the cloth. I sense a feeling of warmth and comfort, mixed with a hint of fear, but nothing overwhelming or powerful enough to pull me into Dominguez's mind. It's disappointing but not unexpected.

My finger still bleeding, I reach for another article of clothing, hoping for the familiar tug of Reading to draw me in. But like the first shirt, there's nothing more than a vague sense of comfort and warmth. The jeans are the same.

"Well, this is a bust," I say, reaching for the pair of shoes, the last items on the table I haven't touched.

But as soon as I place my bloody fingertip to the side of the shoe, there's a familiar pull in the pit of my stomach, and I gasp.

"Wait," I say, fighting the Reading. "I'm getting something. Fuck. Get a notepad."

Cross, clearly caught off guard by my outburst, fumbles for his pocket and pulls his notepad out.

"I'll be right back," I say through gritted teeth, and then I let go.

Others in the gang, they equate their worth with their appearance. They spend their money on designer clothes, on the newest pair of Yeezys, on gold and ice that they loop around their necks like nooses. It's all about how they look, how they behave. They've gotta be the toughest guys, the meanest assholes, the last ones to back down from a fight.

But not you. As you stare down at your shoes—a pair your mama bought you when you graduated from high school, tears in her eyes as she called you smart and handsome, her pride in you like morning light on her face—and their scuffed and torn surface, you know that what you're doing is different. What you're doing has real worth, *real* value. It's not for show. No performance here. No, you're about to do something that'll make a change in the world, have some real fucking impact. You're done playing at being a man. Now, you're going to be one.

Not that anyone else is going to see it that way. Not Cisco, not Martín, not any of the guys you call your friends, your brothers. They won't understand why you made this decision, how that dead kid changed everything. It's one more body, right? Who cares?

But the news uses the same picture of him in every report. Every time, they plaster a smiling school portrait across the screen. The kid's missing his front teeth, and the gap is visible as he grins at the photographer. His red polo is unbuttoned and uneven, but the kid doesn't seem to care. He's full of life, of excitement, and whenever you see his face, you see your kid brother smiling back at you instead.

They said it was an accident. Said that they didn't see the kid, didn't aim at him anyway. They blamed a child for being in the line of fire, and you gritted your teeth and nodded, pretending to understand even though you didn't.

But you're done pretending. You know things. You have information that can stop something like this from happening again. It's stored in your mind from years spent with this extended, twisted family that your heart wants to love and hate in equal measure. More than that, you know about the corruption that's soaked into the cops like a stain, dyeing them black and gold.

Not all of them have been tainted, though. You flip a business card over in your fingers, taking in the Chicago Police Department logo and a name printed in embossed ink. The letters are raised beneath your fingertips, the card bent and worn from hours spent worrying it like a favorite blanket, like a source of comfort.

And though your heart is pounding, and your hands sweat as you pick up the pay phone, you dial the number with steady fingers.

"Detective Carlos Martinez," he says.

You take a breath, hold it as you consider the consequences of this action. But then you remember a gap-toothed smile and you exhale.

"I want to talk."

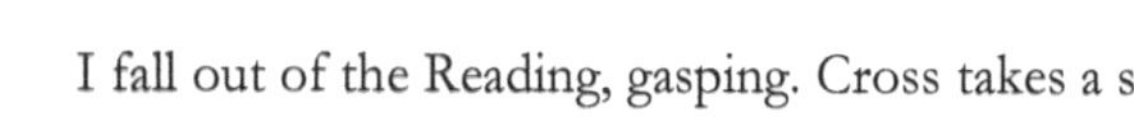

I fall out of the Reading, gasping. Cross takes a step toward me, but I hold up a hand, stopping him.

"I'm all right," I pant. "I'm just… he was terrified, and it's messing with me."

Cross doesn't say anything and watches as I slowly regain my composure. After a moment, he speaks.

"What'd you learn?"

"Nothing new, not really." I shake my head. "He was upset about the kid, like Martinez said, and he wanted to do something about it. He was conflicted about it but thought he was doing the right thing."

"Anything about the dirty cop?"

I shake my head again. "No. He knew there were police working for the Latin Kings and that Martinez wasn't one of them. But that's it. If he knew more than that, he wasn't thinking about it in the memory I Read."

The chair across from me squeaks against the floor as Cross pulls it back from the table and sits heavily. "What're you going to bleed on next, then?"

Pushing the shoe away from me, I lean back and sigh. "I don't know, but I don't know what else we can do. We haven't gotten anywhere with interviews, there's almost no evidence, and there's at least one police officer in *our own district* who's going to want to stop us from getting anywhere with what little we have."

Cross sighs and rubs the bridge of his nose. "We're going to be good investigators," he says with patience. "We're going to work with the evidence we have. We're going to interview the victim's known acquaintances. And we sure as hell aren't going to let some gangbanging cop stop us from figuring out who killed that CI."

He reaches for my hand, not caring about the blood smeared across my skin as he squeezes it. "I know it's frustrating. I'm frustrated, too. I hate that there are cops mixed up in all of this. But we'll figure it out. We've just started working the case. There's still time to catch these assholes. But we don't let our emotions get the better of us. We're analytical. We're in control. And we're better than them because of it. Okay?"

After a moment, I nod. "Okay. Sorry." I pull my hand back and gesture toward the shoe. "I'm still sorting through what he was feeling. He wanted to make a difference even though he knew it wouldn't make any sense to his friends. It's still rattling around in me."

"Did he mention anyone specifically?"

I frown, sifting through the jumbled memory still bouncing through my head. "Cisco. Martín." I close my eyes, concentrating. "I think that was it, though."

"We know Cisco is a bust." He gestures toward the door. "Let's go find Martín."

CHAPTER SEVEN

Martín Ortega is about as unassuming of a gangster as I can imagine. He's slightly overweight, though he hides it well with his clothes—a worn and baggy jacket, black shirt that's fitted but not tight, and jeans that taper at the leg. His hair is tidy, a close-cut fade that doesn't look like it requires much maintenance. Thick glasses are perched on his nose, and as he reads a newspaper while sitting on a park bench, he looks like a mild-mannered young man enjoying a quiet moment to himself. I have to look over his rap sheet again, confused by what I'm seeing on paper and what I'm seeing in person.

On paper, Ortega is far from mild-mannered. He has multiple counts of assault and battery. A short stint at the MCC for *aggravated* battery. There's a pending case out for him on yet *another* assault. But looking at him now, you wouldn't think he'd hurt a fly. Honestly, it doesn't look like he *could.*

"It's always the quiet ones," Cross says to me from our vantage point across the park.

It took us a few hours to track this guy down. Though we had plenty of other names to check, Cross and I decided to focus on the people Dominguez knew best. Ortega's name had come up in the Reading, and the emotion that had tangled around his name like vines was sharp and hot with betrayal, regret, and a twisted love.

Dominguez was conflicted about what he was doing, about betraying his found family for the sake of the Greater Good—his emphasis, not mine. I'm still grappling with the remains of his guilt, the low churn in my gut not making the pending confrontation any easier.

"So, how do you want to play this?" I ask Cross, tamping down on the echo of Dominguez's emotions.

"I'm still trying to figure that out." He looks at me with concern in his green gaze. "Any ideas would be appreciated."

There's no way Ortega is going to talk to us. We're two cops he doesn't know, asking questions about his dead friend and blood brother. Considering he's out on bail currently, he has no reason to possibly incriminate himself in this bullshit.

There's only one reason he'd talk to the cops, and as I think it, a shiver races up my spine. "I… might have an idea."

"Oh?" Cross asks, sounding suspicious.

I nod. "Follow my lead?"

"Oh God." He runs a hand over his face and looks at me again, brow furrowed. "I don't like the sound of that."

"Do you trust me?"

"*Not* helping, Phillips." He lets out a slow breath. "But yes."

"Okay. I'm going to make him think we're in on it."

Cross's brow goes from furrowed to raised in a second. "What now?"

"Martinez doesn't know how big the ring is, right?" I tilt my head toward Ortega. "How much you want to bet he doesn't, either?"

"So, you're going to pretend you're dirty."

"I'm going to pretend that *we're* dirty." I gesture between us. "Partners, right?"

He sighs, and it sounds pained. "Partners. Jesus Christ, Kim."

"It'll be fine. Stay close."

I start walking toward Ortega and pull my badge out from where it's tucked into my jacket. The chain rattles against the zipper, and the heavy metal shield bounces against my chest with every step. Close on my heels, Cross pulls his badge out, too.

The park is, unsurprisingly, empty. It's a cold April afternoon. The sky is overcast, dense and bloated with clouds that inch their way over the city. Every few minutes, an icy wind picks up and rustles through trees that haven't decided whether they should bud or not. A few have made the plunge, and specks of green cling to the ends of their branches in hopeful flecks of color. The trees shiver as the wind races over their limbs, and I join them as the snap of cold finds its way beneath my collar and into the warm cocoon of my jacket.

You're sure this is a good idea? Priya asks as she hovers near my shoulder.

Not really, but I don't have a better one.

She frowns. *Maybe arrest him, bring him into an interrogation room, and make him talk like a normal detective?*

You think I'm normal? I shoot her a sideways glance. *Since when?*

Okay, fair point. Still, this seems a little… underhanded.

There's nothing that says we have to tell a suspect the truth. Now hush. You're going to distract me.

Ortega's body tenses as we approach, but he doesn't look up from his newspaper. He flips to the next page idly, unconcerned. When Cross and I stop in front of him, he continues looking down. I don't say anything but take on a graceless stance, hand on my hip, and wait.

Eventually, Ortega glances up at me over the rim of his glasses, one dark eyebrow raised in question.

"Can I help you, Officers?"

I let a slow smile creep its way across my face. "Detectives, and maybe you can, Martín."

He freezes when I say his name. "Do I know you?"

"No, but I know you." I let my smile become predatory. "What're you reading about, Martín?"

He ignores my question. "What do you want?"

"Oh, nothing really," I say before sitting next to him on the bench. I throw my arms over the back of it, letting my hands dangle, and cross my legs as I get comfortable. "But you'll want to watch that attitude. Don't want anything to… happen."

"Are you threatening me?"

I laugh. "We don't need to threaten you, Ortega. Just like we didn't need to threaten Dominguez."

He barks out a laugh. "I don't know anyone named Dominguez."

"Really?" Cross folds his arms in front of his chest and stares down at Ortega. "No idea who Juan Dominguez is?"

"Never heard of him before."

"That's not what our bosses said." I look at my nails, affecting nonchalance. "And they sure said a lot about you."

"There's no fucking way you had anything to do with Dominguez." Ortega's voice wavers a little, and I smell blood in the water.

"You know that for a fact?" I look at Cross and grin. It's just this edge of sane, and I know I'm playing it up, but I need to sell this shit. "Looks like we've got Sherlock fucking Holmes over here. Solving all sorts of mysteries in Chicago." I turn back to Ortega, fighting to keep the manic light in my eyes bright. "Wonder if you'd like to solve the mystery of how four bullets ended up in Dominguez's back while two detectives were watching him."

As he quickly glances between Cross and me, his gaze slides from combative to wary. After a beat, he folds up his newspaper and sets it on the bench between us. When he asks this time, the question is less a challenge and more a capitulation. "What do you want?"

"We just want to talk… for now." I look at Cross. "Isn't that right?"

He nods. "We've got a few questions about our mutual friend, may he rest in peace."

"Okay, fine," Ortega spits. "Ask your fucking questions."

"Who's talking about Dominguez?" Cross asks.

"Fuck, everyone." He laughs without humor. "No one saw it coming."

Neither did Dominguez, I think.

Ortega continues. "I shouldn't have been surprised, though. He's been jumpy for weeks. I thought it was because of that money drop that went bad, but I guess it was about something else."

"What do you think it was about?" I ask.

He frowns at me. "Don't you already know?"

"We need to know what *you* know," Cross says, saving my ass. "Now talk."

"First, there was that drop a month ago that went sideways. Then, he got caught by some cops with weed on him. He knew better than that. Your guys got him out, but they weren't happy about that shit. Dude kept making trouble for himself, you know? I didn't think he'd get killed for it, but he must've fucked up real bad." He eyes us as if we'll tell him more. When we stay silent, he looks away, pushing his glasses up his nose. "They don't like it when you fuck with the cash. But that's all I know. People are talking, but that's shock. It'll die down in a few days."

Cross meets my eyes, then nods. "And that's it?"

"That's it," Ortega confirms. "Can I go now, Officers?"

The title sounds like a curse as it falls from his mouth. I fight a grimace. "Yeah, you can go."

He picks his newspaper up, folds it into thirds, and tucks it under his arm. "Hope I don't see you again."

"Feeling's mutual," I say to his retreating back. Once he rounds a corner and disappears from sight, I curse. "Dominguez got picked up for drugs?"

"Sounds like we should have an arrest record for that," Cross says with a glint in his eyes. "What are the chances that our dirty cop left some fingerprints on the paperwork?"

I stand and roll my shoulders. "No idea, but it's something. We should look into the money drop that Ortega mentioned, too. If it went bad, there might be a report about it, and if there was money involved, it might've been seized."

We walk back to our cruiser, then boot up the simple laptop that's fastened on a movable arm on the center dash. I type in Dominguez's name and kick myself slightly for not thinking to check his record more thoroughly earlier. I blame it on shock and sleep deprivation, but I still feel pretty stupid. After a moment, the arrest for two-point-eight grams of marijuana shows up.

"He was busted in the Sixth," I tell Cross. "Misdemeanor drug possession. They tossed him in lockup, but then he was released." I curse. "There's nothing here about why, though. Shit."

"Who're the arresting officers?"

I scan the file. "Carter and Lawson. You know them?"

"I've talked to Lawson before. I can give her a call, see if she remembers the arrest."

"And I'll see if I can figure out what this drop was about. You figure it's in the Seventh?"

Cross nods. "I have a feeling they were keeping their major activity to territory they knew they'd be safe in. Might be why Dominguez got picked up in the Sixth. And Ortega said it was a month ago. That should make it easier to track down."

"It can't hurt," I say as I buckle in. "Still, there's gonna be a lot of paperwork to dig through. Better to get this show on the road now instead of waiting around here."

Cross pulls onto the street, and I start typing into the cruiser's laptop, seeing if anything comes up when I search for the rough outline of what we know. It's not looking too promising—there are twenty pages of results, and I quietly curse to myself.

About halfway back to District HQ, my phone rings, distracting me from my fruitless search. Banks's name flashes at me from the screen, and I sigh before hanging up.

"Who was that?" Cross asks, his eyes still trained on the road.

"Banks." I sound irritated and try to push the feeling down. "She's been calling me for a couple of days."

"You don't want to talk to her? I thought you two had become friends somewhat."

I roll my eyes. "Friends might be a bit strong."

"Still, I thought you liked her."

She's avoiding Andi, Priya offers, *because Kim doesn't like what she's going to say.*

"What's she going to say?"

I sigh. "She wants to talk about that energy we've been tracking."

Cross glances at me for a moment, then looks back at the road. "Seems like something worth talking about, considering."

"Yeah," I agree, sulking a little, "but we haven't gotten anywhere with it since January."

"I thought it was going better than that." He sounds surprised.

"We know it's everywhere death is. We also know that ghosts that come in contact with it are more likely to Turn and do so at a faster pace than usual." I rub the bridge of my nose. "*Unless* they're like Dave and are protecting one of those focal points. But we don't know how it's created or where it comes from, and we don't know how to get rid of it, only contain it, and we don't know *why* ghosts like Dave aren't affected by it."

Cross shakes his head. "He hasn't been able to

help?"

"Yes and no," I say, thinking of the ghost haunting the monument at Oak Woods Cemetery. "He's shown us how to set up new focal points, which keeps that shit contained, but he doesn't know any more than we do. Honestly, I think I need to talk to the people running the show to get a real handle on this."

"But that's not happening," Cross says seriously.

Dave won't budge on it, Priya Sends to both of us. *Other than Ruth Peterson, he hasn't given us any names. Says he hasn't been authorized to do more than that.*

"And Taka keeps saying he doesn't know anything about the group. When I've pressed him to get us a meeting with Peterson, he hasn't been able to."

Cross raises his eyebrows before turning right. "Not even after three months of trying?"

"Nope. As her receptionist has told me time and time again, she's booked solid until the summer. The earliest opening she has is at the beginning of June."

"So, another ten weeks."

I nod, and the car falls silent.

I don't mention the other mystery hanging over our heads: Cross's burgeoning—and inexplicable—powers. They've been growing, slowly but steadily, over the intervening months. There haven't been any more light shows like when I first warded him, but he's falling into Second-Sight and Sending easier and easier every day. Part of me wants to put it down to practice and his new mentor. Cross is, if nothing else, dedicated and focused in everything he puts his mind to. But this feels like something else. His powers flare around me, and anytime I look at him in Second-Sight, the scar in the center of his chest burns with a low, golden flame that I can see through his shirt. What used to be a temporary thing is now constant.

The change—and the scar—don't seem to bother him, though, and the random spikes in his powers have evened out. I, on the other hand, find myself drawn to that glow. Like a cat with a sunbeam, I want to roll around in it, to press against his light and soak it into my body. It pulls me in as much as he does, and I find myself conflicted by that gentle, but irresistible, attraction. I want to give in but know I shouldn't.

His warm hand on top of mine breaks me from my thoughts. He gives it a gentle squeeze. "We'll figure it out, Kim."

I turn and smile at him, my chest swelling with a warmth that overwhelms me. He always seems to know when I need these little touches, these reminders that I'm not alone in this fight. Flipping my hand so our palms are pressed together, I tangle my fingers with his.

"I know." I give his hand an answering squeeze. "I'm just frustrated."

"At least it's not getting worse."

He has a point. I sigh. "I'll keep pushing Taka to get a meeting set up with Ruth. Maybe he can convince her to find an opening for us."

Not that Taka's been forthcoming with information about Peterson. But he'll help me if I ask, I know it. Or, at least, I'm pretty sure he will.

Probably.

Ugh.

CHAPTER EIGHT

I let out a sigh as Cross turns into the parking lot in front of District HQ. While I've never been a fan of looking through records, at least the impending dive into the computer system for this money drop gone bad will keep my mind occupied. Spinning my wheels on all of this supernatural bullshit is going to burn me out. Some good old-fashioned police work will help me re-center myself, get focused.

Avoidance is a coping mechanism for a reason.

Cross and I get to it as soon as we sit at our desks. He gives Lawson a call while I start sifting through arrest reports, looking for anything that could be the money drop Ortega mentioned. But even after an hour and a half of searching, I can't come up with anything. There are more than a few notes about money seized, but nothing that seems to fit with a drug op gone bad, and Dominguez's name is nowhere to be found. After I widen the date range on my search, thinking that Ortega might have misremembered when this thing happened, I'm flooded with so many cases there's no way I'll get through them all tonight. I lean back in my chair, which lets out a squeal that barely covers my groan.

Exhaustion rides me hard. It's not night yet, though the sky is darkening when I glance out the front doors. Cross and I have been up for at least thirty-six hours at this point. My eyes are sore and gritty from staring at a computer screen, and the tedious, mind-numbing review hasn't helped me stay awake. I stretch, my chair letting out a plaintive squeak that I feel a kinship with, and wait for Cross to look up from his computer.

If he's tired, it doesn't show. He's in the zone. His call with Lawson ended at least an hour ago, and his eyes have been glued to his computer screen since, his fingers racing over his keyboard as he does whatever it is that he's doing.

"What've you got?" I ask, hoping to break his concentration.

He hums at me and keeps his eyes on his screen. "What, Phillips?"

"What did Lawson have to say? What've you been doing for the last hour?"

He types a little more, then pulls his hands away from the keyboard, frowning at them like errant children. "Well, not much." He leans back. "First, she remembers Dominguez. His tattoos, specifically. He had a fresh one, and when they cuffed him, it bled through his shirt."

"Why'd they bust him?"

He laughs. "He was standing on a street corner, smoking a joint. Didn't even try to hide it. She said it was like he was trying to get in trouble."

"Why would he do that?" I frown. "You'd think he

would take a low profile, try to stay inconspicuous."

"Yeah, you'd think." Cross shakes his head. "Instead, he blew smoke in Carter's face and nearly got tased for it."

"Jesus."

I know Carter, and he's not a small guy. Older, with thinning hair and a beer belly that hangs over his duty belt, he's well over six feet tall and has arms that ripple with muscles. Last I remember, he was playing on a rec hockey league and got in trouble at least once for starting a fight on the ice.

If you were going to blow smoke in someone's face, his was not the one to choose.

"So, what? They pick him up for drug possession, book him, and then he disappears?"

"Pretty much," Cross says with a frown. "Lawson's shift ended, and when she came in the next day, Dominguez had been released."

"That's helpful. You think Martinez would be able to tell us more?"

"I don't think he was surveilling Dominguez yet, so he may not have even known about it—not unless he looked up Dominguez's record or Dominguez told him."

"So, it's another dead end."

"Not entirely. We know that Dominguez was trying to draw attention to himself. Maybe he was baiting someone, trying to force their hand."

"Getting arrested on a misdemeanor is one way to

do that, I guess." I sigh. "I couldn't find shit on this money thing, though."

"Nothing?" Cross sags in his seat. "Damn, I was hoping you'd get something. These records don't say anything about who released him, either."

"So, what do we do next?"

Cross gives me a tired grin. "Grab dinner and go to bed?"

I check the clock. It's just shy of 5:00 p.m., and honestly, a burger and sleep sound amazing. As I'm about to tell him to grab his coat, my computer chimes merrily with an email notification. I glance at Outlook, then let out a long breath.

"Prelim autopsy report is in," I say.

Cross looks at his computer and joins me with a sigh. "Guess we're going to have to put a pin in dinner."

"Seems like."

While the prelim report is pretty basic, it's clear about a couple of things. Dominguez died within twelve to sixteen hours of us finding him, and death had been almost instantaneous. One of the four bullets hit his aortic arch and caused a "critical aortic dissection," the largest artery in his body shredded like tissue paper, with blood filling his chest in seconds. It's obviously a homicide, but the immediate cause of death is listed as hypovolemic shock and exsanguination. There's an additional note that the medical examiner found unburnt black powder residue on Dominguez's clothing.

I frown. "His killer was close enough to leave gunpowder on his clothes, but the kid didn't turn around when the attacker approached? Why isn't he looking to see who's walking up to him?"

"It's strange," Cross agrees.

"You think…" I pause, considering. "You think he *knew* his killer?"

"That still doesn't answer why he didn't turn around. Even if someone I knew approached me from behind, I wouldn't leave my back to them."

I raise an eyebrow. "You worried about anything, Cross?"

"No." He shakes his head. "But I'd want to talk to the person, right? Say hi? Shake their hand? Something? It's odd that he'd leave his back open like that."

"We're missing something here, and I don't know what it is." I push back from my desk, frustrated and tired. "What aren't we seeing?"

"Kim," Cross says, eyes soft. "Maybe we should get some rest, let this sit until tomorrow? We're going nowhere right now, and it's not going to get better if we keep pushing."

"No." I shake my head and stand. "No, we're going down to the morgue, and we're going to look at his body. I can Read it, maybe get something useful from it."

He frowns at me. "What do you mean Read it?"

I still. I haven't told him about Reading his memories that day in the graveyard. Though the memory lingers like an invasion and I've wanted to tell him, I haven't figured out how to broach the subject.

Hey, you know how you passed out that one time because a deranged ghost tried to murder you? Well, while you were unconscious, I relived one of your memories, one where you wanted me, and I totally knew you had a thing for me before you said or did anything about it. Sorry about the gross violation of your privacy!

He continues looking at me, brow furrowed in confusion.

"Maybe," I say quickly, trying to cover up the awkward pause in conversation. "Maybe I can Read something from his body. We invest emotional energy in our bodies, right? Why couldn't I Read something from Dominguez's?"

"It's certainly an idea," he says hesitantly. "Are you sure you're up to it? Readings seem to take a lot out of you."

"You can get me home if I need help, right?" I ask, forcing an upbeat tone to my voice that only has his frown deepening.

"Yeah, I can do that." He stands and reaches for his coat, which is hanging over the back of his chair. "But you're sure you're okay? You're acting a little weird right now."

"I'm just tired," I say, and it's both the truth and a lie.

I'm exhausted. Keeping this secret from Cross is exhausting. Trying to figure out how in the hell he developed the Sight is exhausting. Hunting down focal points and Turned ghosts and mysterious, secret organizations is exhausting. The exhaustion I feel from this case and its tedium feels like a relief. At least it's straightforward, even with its complexities.

"You can drive," I say. "I'll grab a nap on the way over."

I take the easy out and shut my eyes as soon as Cross pulls out of the parking lot. I mean to fake sleep, but I'm dragged under almost immediately, the darkness and the quiet sound of the road beneath our tires lulling me into an easy, dreamless doze. Cross shakes me awake, and I blink at the Cook County Medical Examiner's sign.

"You sure you can handle this?" he asks, giving me a long, steady look. "We can wait until tomorrow."

I rub my eyes and push the car door open. "Yeah, I'm fine. Let's go."

It's after business hours, and the waiting room is empty. At least, it's empty of the living. Cross tenses next to me. I give him a quizzical look and take in the waiting room.

There's a man nearby with a knife sticking out of his head, blood leaking from around the hilt. A woman with gunshot wounds spread across her chest stands on the other side of him, her shaking hands pressed to the still-bleeding wounds. Another woman's eyes bulge out, her throat ringed with bruises shaped like fingers. There's a man missing an arm and a young child, mouth frothy and eyes glazed.

It's a little grisly, sure, but it's normal. I've been

seeing ghosts like these since I was a kid. I'm used to it, unmoved by the death surrounding us.

"Have they…" He swallows. "Have they always been here?"

I look around, taking in the many dead crowding the room. "I don't recognize most of them, which means they're new, but yeah, it always looks like this."

"Jesus." He lets the words out on a long breath. "How do you handle it?"

I shrug. "You get used to it in time. And these ones tend to pass quickly. They're harmless."

He side-eyes the man with the knife sticking out of his head. "You're sure we don't need to worry about that energy stuff? I thought it was drawn to death."

"It is," I agree, "but this death is… transitional. The bodies—and the ghosts—don't stay here for long. I'm pretty sure the ME has a Burner on the payroll for when it gets too crowded, too. Cemeteries are way worse. They don't really worry about ghosts hanging around."

"I guess. Still… it's a little upsetting, don't you think?"

"It can be, sure, but like I said, you adjust. Drop out of Second-Sight. You'll be fine."

Cross doesn't look convinced, but I can tell that he follows my suggestion when the tight line of his shoulders eases. We walk to the receptionist's desk and press the buzzer. A few moments later, a receptionist appears, frowning.

"It's after business hours," she says before eyeing

our badges, "Officers."

"We're here to see Dr. Abramo," I say. "He just sent over a preliminary autopsy report, and we need to do some follow-up."

She frowns but picks up the phone next to her computer. "One moment, please."

After dialing a number, she turns her shoulder to us, speaking quietly into the handset. She glances at us, then nods before hanging up.

"He'll meet you in the first autopsy bay down the hall."

Cross murmurs a thanks, and we head in the direction she pointed. As we push our way inside the first room, Dr. Abramo looks up from where he's taking notes at a table along the far wall.

"Detectives," he says as the doors swing shut behind us. "I have to admit, I didn't think I'd hear from you tonight."

"What can you tell us about Dominguez?"

He finishes making a note, then closes his folder and looks at us. "Well, other than what's in the prelim report, not much. The aortic arch was destroyed completely, and he bled out within moments. It was a rather catastrophic injury."

"Can we see the body?"

Abramo frowns. "We've already processed it. Forensics has the evidence from the corpse, along with the clothes and personal possessions. I know it's a preliminary report, but the external examination is complete. If you need details about the condition of the body, it's all there."

"I need to look for something," I say. "Something you won't be able to see."

"Ah." Abramo picks up his folder and starts walking toward the door. "I understand, Detective. It'll take me a few minutes to get him out of storage. Wait here."

As soon as Abramo leaves the room, the door swinging shut behind him, Cross turns to me. "So, now what?"

"Now, we wait."

"And you try something completely untested while exhausted and, in the process, likely contaminate evidence."

"You heard Abramo," I huff. "They've already processed the body."

"That doesn't mean he's performed the internal examination, though." Cross runs a hand through his hair. "This feels reckless, Kim. There's got to be another option."

I throw my hands up. "Well, you tell me what that is, then. As far as we know, any evidence linking Dominguez to this dirty cop—or cops—has been cleaned up. He's got access to our records. He knows how to cover his tracks. But he can't cover up Dominguez's memories. There's no way to wipe those from the system. And," I add, finger pointed at him, "Lieutenant Walker already cleared me to use my powers to solve this. So why shouldn't I?"

He takes a step toward me, his voice lower. "She doesn't know you're anything more than a Burner. A *Burner* wouldn't be using their blood to try to get more information out of a corpse. And even if you *do* get something usable from this exercise, how are we going to get it into evidence without revealing that you've got more going on with you than is strictly normal? This big secret is going to come out."

"We can fudge it, say I scribed a circle to do the Reading."

"So, you want to lie."

I stiffen. "I want to solve this, and I want to keep us safe. Don't forget, I'm not the only one here with secrets."

After a long moment, Cross looks away, his jaw tight and his expression unreadable. "It's clear I'm not going to be able to stop you, but I think this is a bad idea. You're taking a risk you don't need to take." He scrubs a hand over his face, then gestures toward the door. "I thought that you could only Read off of inanimate objects, anyway, not people."

Technically, Priya offers awkwardly, *a corpse is an inanimate object.*

"Not the point," Cross says with a slight frown.

You should tell him, Priya says softly.

I should not.

You really should.

"What should you do?" Cross asks.

I curse. *Can you keep it down? Stop broadcasting.*

I didn't! Priya glares. *I kept it between you and me, I swear.*

"Kim." He says my name with suspicion. "What's going on?"

I glance at Priya, hoping for help. She gives me a pained smile, then disappears.

Traitor!

Body tense, I turn to Cross. "I may have Read a memory from someone before."

"You did?" His eyebrows go up. "So, that's why you know you can do it?"

"Yes."

Thank God, he doesn't ask whose memory I Read.

"Who was it?"

Son of a bitch.

I'm normally a good liar. I do it as part of my job all of the time. During suspect interviews, I can play perps like finely tuned musical instruments, plucking information from them with a virtuosic talent. I lied to my parents for years about the ghosts I saw. Lied to myself about my attraction to Cross, my supposed independence, my lack of need for other people. I'm a more-than-proficient liar.

But not today. Today, I'm tired and worn thin. Today, I open my mouth to speak, then close it, gaping like a fish as I try to think of who in the hell I would've gotten close enough to Read a memory from. Today, before I can say anything, understanding sparks in Cross's eyes.

"You Read something from me"—his gaze

narrows—"and you didn't tell me about it?"

"It's… complicated."

"What's complicated about it?"

I flush. "I was in your head, Cross. It was personal."

"All the more reason you should've told me." His eyes harden. "What did you see?"

"I don't want to talk about this here."

"You clearly didn't want to talk about it at *all*, Phillips. So, spill. What did you see?"

I stumble over my words, but before I can make sense from the tangle of syllables falling from my mouth, Abramo backs his way into the room, a gurney with a body bag on it trailing behind.

"We'll talk later," I say. Cross's eyes glint with banked irritation. "I promise."

"I'm going to hold you to that." He turns to Abramo. "Thank you for bringing him in here."

"Of course, of course." He gives me a quick smile. "Anything for our resident Medium."

"I'm going to have to put a bit of blood on him," I say with a wince.

Abramo's eyebrow lifts before he turns around and pulls open a drawer. He reaches inside and pulls out a surgical marking pen, then passes me the purple marker. I take it, slightly confused.

"Mark where you're going to be doing your bleeding, Detective. That way we know where it came from."

I put a glove on my right hand before unzipping the body bag. I pull it far enough back that I can see

Dominguez's face and upper torso. The four entry wounds are small, tight circles of red in his flesh, ringed with black. I make a careful circle on his shoulder above the last of his tattoos. Then, I lean down and pull my knife from my boot. The silver is cold against my palm, even through the thin layer of nitrile. It stings when I press the blade through the scarred skin of my fingertip, and I watch as blood beads on the blade.

After a deep breath, I press my bloodied thumb to the center of the small, purple circle on Dominguez's skin. There's a rush, and I'm pulled under, dragged into the memories of a dead man.

CHAPTER NINE

Your hands are shaking. They haven't done that in years, not since you were promoted from the corner to the car, running money from dealers to the people in charge. But today, the duffel full of cash clenched in your fists trembles. The weight of it drags you down. Your arms strain and your shoulders ache. Sweat trickles down the valley between your shoulder blades to pool at the small of your back. It's hot and itchy and you desperately want to do something about it, but you can't.

Your hands are so full.

You've been here before, though. So many times over the years, you've been in this place or some other place like it. An infinite reflection of dingy, run-down buildings. There are doors that you will walk through and people you will talk to, and throughout it all, your mind will be blank and quiet because that's what it has to be if you're going to make it through this.

"Hey man," Martín says, nudging your shoulder to get your attention. "You okay?"

You stammer over words that you can't remember, but it seems to be enough. He nods at you, brow furrowed and eyes shadowed, and, together, you walk inside.

It's dark. There are a few lights, but not many. Squinting, you take careful steps farther into the bowels of this anonymous building. They ring out around you like quiet shots. You wonder when the bullets will hit, when those sounds will bounce back and kill you.

Something's going to, and soon. You know it is. It's why your hands shake, why your back sweats. There are eyes on you, watching from the darkness, watching from the man who says he's your friend, watching from the others who say they're your family. You don't know how it happened, but somehow, someone knows. They haven't said anything, but you can sense it in the way they talk to you, in the way they move. Their darting glances, those eyes that watch you wherever you go. Your secret is out, and there's a timer on your life.

A deadline, in the truest sense.

But your life isn't due tonight. This isn't when you die. Like you know that they're coming for you, you know when they'll arrive. There's fear twisting in your gut, but mixed with it is certainty. You know when Santa Muerte will come for you and it's not today.

Finally, you and Martín reach the end of the hallway. There's an office, its door shut and muted light shining from the cracks. He gives you a nod. You aren't sure what he's trying to tell you with the motion, if he's offering comfort or saying goodbye. Before you can figure it out, his hand is on the knob, and he's pushing the door open.

The light blinds you. There's a spotlight or some shit like it pointed straight at the door. Martín curses and throws his arm up over his eyes, but your hands are full and heavy and shaking, and you can't block the light. Tears sting your eyes, and you blink them away and squint into the brightness.

"What the fuck?" Martín asks. "Quit fucking with us and turn that fucking thing off."

His temper is rising, and with it, the small hairs on the back of your neck. Martín is far from gentle when he's mad. You've seen him break people like glass, watched him shatter their minds and bodies as if they meant nothing.

You feel your clock ticking. This isn't the time for violence.

"It's fine. Let's do this."

You toss the duffel forward. It's heavy, so it doesn't go far, sliding only a few inches across the dusty, stained carpet. There's over a hundred grand in that black bag. You watched each bill run through the counter, banded them yourself in tidy bundles. There's hard work tied up in the tattered canvas. Yours and so many others'. Men in fields in Mexico, women running supplies through the border and North, kids and idiots on the corners, buying and selling in equal portion. Sweat. Tears. Blood. All for that one bag and its tainted contents.

"You're short."

The voice isn't one you've heard before. Neither is the tone. You may hate these people, hate this life, but you're fucking good at it. You're never short.

"You haven't counted it."

"I don't need to." The sound of canvas across cheap carpet. The harsh rasp of a zipper. "You're fucking short."

The sweat down your back turns cold. You're not short. You know it. You counted that shit. You were careful. The last thing you want is to draw attention to yourself. Not now, not here.

The timer ticks down.

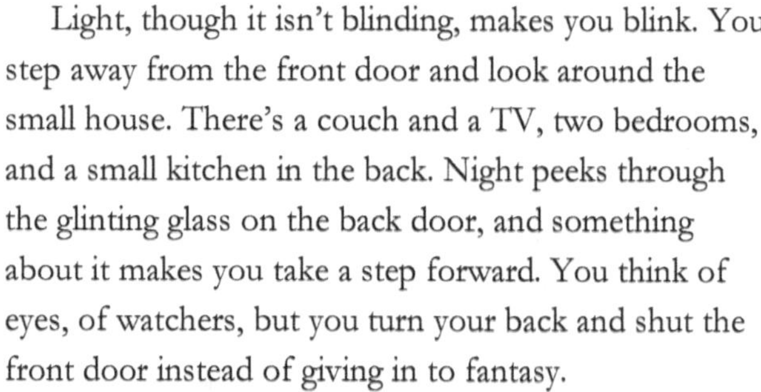

Light, though it isn't blinding, makes you blink. You step away from the front door and look around the small house. There's a couch and a TV, two bedrooms, and a small kitchen in the back. Night peeks through the glinting glass on the back door, and something about it makes you take a step forward. You think of eyes, of watchers, but you turn your back and shut the front door instead of giving in to fantasy.

You've been lucky. Twenty years old, a lifelong member of a clan that is at times as vicious as it is loving, and somehow, you've made it through unscathed. You should've been dead a month ago. You nearly were. But something shifted in that room, enough that you and Martín were able to run, your lives the only thing you left with, pride and dignity forgotten on the cheap carpet as Santa Muerte laughed in the dark.

Martinez has your back now. He's got people watching you, got cops sitting right outside of this house and all the others he's shuffled you through. It's not perfect—there are still cops out there who know and shouldn't—but it's better than the constant paranoia and exhaustion that rode you ever since that drop went bad.

It's better now. You throw your bag into one of the bedrooms, then make the mattress pretending to be a bed with clean sheets and blankets. The pillow is a little thin, but it cradles your head when you lie on it. Breathing seems easier. *Life* seems easier, even though it isn't.

There are still so many more things you have to do to make this sacrifice matter. But until you're sure you'll be safe—that your mom and kid brother will be safe— you aren't giving them a name.

It's three days later, and a knock comes from the back door. You wipe your hands on the towel in the bathroom and yell to whoever is waiting.

"Coming!"

You don't recognize the man at the back door. He's white and tall and stands like he's used to people respecting him for no reason other than a uniform. His hair is hidden beneath a knit cap, and his jacket is leather and dark. His hands are bare and he breathes into them as you stand, frozen in the living room.

Somewhere, a timer ticks.

"Hey, you gonna let me in or what?" he asks through the glass, rubbing his hands together and shifting his weight. "It's fucking freezing out here."

"Yeah," you say, manners moving your feet for you. Your hand opens the door, your voice already polite and welcoming before you can stop it. "Sorry about that."

"No worries," he says with a disarming grin. "Just coming in to check on you. You doing okay?"

"Yeah, I'm settling in." You shift, uncertain what to say next.

"Good, that's good. We're real glad you're doing okay. It's a brave thing you're doing."

You don't know if you agree with the man, but you duck your head and smile self-consciously. You don't feel brave. Fear feels like your best friend these days. It's always there, cheering you on from the sidelines, patting you on the back with hard hands, and smiling at you with skeletal teeth. It watches over you while you sleep, so that when you wake, you're met with its empty eyes, staring back at you from the darkness.

The man reaches out to shake your hand. You take it, and it's still damp with his breath. Part of you flinches from that, an intimacy you weren't expecting and didn't ask for. But another part of you revels in that small reminder of life. Of breath exhaled against skin.

"So, what're you doing tonight?" he asks, looking around the house. "Doing anything fun?"

"No." You let his hand drop. "Just staying in. Got a movie from Redbox."

"That sounds nice."

You turn and head back to the front of the house. The door is still unlocked, and Martinez told you that you had to keep it shut and bolted at all times. It's a security thing, he said. A way to keep you safe.

As you turn the bolt, you hear something behind you click and you freeze. You want to turn around, but your body has turned to stone, to ice, to glass. You can't move, and you're afraid if you do, you'll shatter.

"Look, I don't have anything against you personally, kid," the man says. You only now realize he hadn't told you his name. "But John says this has to be done, and what John says, goes. Do me a favor and take a few steps back from the door."

He's so polite about it that you find your feet moving again, though you don't want them to. You want to stumble, to fall, but you're weighted to the ground like a duffel full of money, and you scrape across the cheap carpet a few inches before he tells you to stop.

"If he thought roughing you up would be enough, that's what we'd do. But he says there's no stopping you, so…"

You hear the familiar click of a slide racking. There's a bullet pointed at you now.

"Again, nothing personal."

One.

Two.

Three.

Four.

There's a tearing pain in your chest. Pressure. You pull your hand to your chest and look down. Blood.

So much blood.

And then falling, your legs giving out beneath you. You crash to the floor like broken glass, your arm trapped beneath you. But you don't care. You can't move.

Everything slows.

A timer ticks.

CHAPTER TEN

I gag and pull myself away from Dominguez's body. There's a large utility sink behind me, and I throw myself toward it, gasping and heaving. My hands clench the sides as I throw up. Bile stings my nose and tears fill my eyes. Cross's hand is on my back, soothing, but all I feel is hot, pouring blood and that awful, jagged pain that radiated through my, no, *his* chest.

"Oh God," I groan, head bent over the sink as I spit. It does nothing to clear the taste of vomit from my mouth or the remembered taste of death on my tongue.

Dominguez's death wasn't anything like Jackie Harris's. Hers, though awful, had been peaceful, quiet. It had broken my heart. But Dominguez's death was so fast, so terrifying. He'd had no time to process what was happening, only enough time to realize…

I can't stop shaking. The echo of those gunshots, the tearing ache in my chest and back, slick blood burning its way through my fingers. I gag again, then spit. My sleeve scrapes against my face as I wipe away tears.

There's a gentle hand on my shoulder, and when I turn, Abramo is holding a small paper cup out to me.

Cross's hand on my back falls away as I meet the medical examiner's eyes.

"Mouthwash," he explains, tilting the cup so I can see the light blue liquid sloshing inside. "You're not the first person to throw up here."

I take it from him gratefully and swish it around in my mouth. The mint stings but wipes away the remembered iron tang of blood. I spit again, then turn on the water to wash the mouthwash and my vomit down the drain.

"You okay?" Cross asks.

I can tell he wants to reach for me, to offer me the comfort of his arms wrapped around my body. His hands are by his sides now, though I can still feel the heavy weight of his palm where it rubbed soothing circles against my back. His eyes dig into me, and I feel his concern like a gunshot.

It's too much right now. I close my eyes and try to remember instead.

"I saw his shooter," I say. My body feels distant, and something starts tugging me back into the Reading. It plays out behind my eyes, everything outlined in fiery red light. "I don't know who he is, but I know I've seen him before."

"Police?" The word is heavy on Cross's tongue, and it falls between us with the inexorable pull of gravity.

"I think so." I swallow and open my eyes to meet his. "Yes."

"We'll need to get personnel records," he says,

sounding defeated. "Start looking through ID pictures until you find him."

God, I don't want it to be true. I know that Martinez wouldn't have put us on this if it were a wild goose chase. He wouldn't be investigating officers if he didn't have cause, and he certainly wouldn't have told us about it. But a part of me held out hope that he was wrong, that there was some kind of mistake.

Being a police officer has defined my adult life, and I take pride in the title and the work that I do. I know we aren't perfect, that there are some officers who have done—or will do—terrible things because of power. But to kill someone in cold blood, to take their life when it's our responsibility, our *duty*, to protect and serve… Nausea knots my stomach, and I close my eyes, hoping the darkness will ease the ache.

Instead, I see a man's face in my mind, hear his voice, know the recoil of his gun as it roars through the tiny entryway of that house. The sound is achingly familiar as it ricochets in my mind.

It sounds like my own weapon.

"Do you need anything else, Detectives?" Abramo asks, breaking the long silence.

I open my eyes and shake my head, unable to respond. Cross steps forward.

"We'll call you if we do. Email us the final report when you have it?"

"Of course. Have a good night."

Abramo closes the body bag around Dominguez's

body, then wheels it out of the room. The door closes behind him with a quiet swish, and then Cross is pulling me against his body, his arms tight and strong.

"I've got you," he says into my hair, and I shudder.

"Jesus Christ," I whisper into his chest. "It was fucking awful. So much worse than Jackie. I just…"

"I know," he murmurs. "I'm here. You're okay."

I shake apart in his arms, though I don't cry. My chest is too tight for it. But I'm racked by trembling shivers that threaten to tear me apart. After long, gasping minutes, the tremors slow and stop. I'm left with Cross's arms tight around my body, my head pressed to the center of his chest, his scar a pulsing warmth that I can feel through his clothes. I dig my fingers into its ridges, trace the shape of it, and watch as my power curls around as if it were a cat, seeking comfort in the sun.

I pull away, though part of me wants to stay safe there until I no longer hear those four sharp echoes in my mind. He lets his hands trail over my arms, his touch turning to a gentle, comforting caress as he steps away.

"Let's get back," he says quietly. "Start looking through records."

I groan, unhappy that we're going to be spending the night sifting through personnel reports. After spending the day reading files and doing research, the thought of more work makes me want to hide in the back seat of our cruiser and stay there until someone makes me come out. As much as I'd rather go home and curl into the safety of my bed and the warmth of Cross's body against mine, I know we can't sit on this. The man's face is fresh in my mind, and the burning ember of anger and disgust won't let me rest until I know his name.

I pull away from my thoughts. Instead, I force myself to relive Dominguez's memory, afraid to look too closely at it but unwilling to let the details slip away. I hear the sharp crack of gunfire, and I frown.

"You know, it's funny."

Cross gives me a puzzled look. "What do you mean?"

"The killer didn't use a silencer or anything like that. He just shot Dominguez, didn't even try to hide it. If there had been a surveillance team sitting outside the house, there's no way they didn't hear those shots. Hell, if we're lucky, a POD picked it up, too."

Cross's expression becomes contemplative. "You think the team was in on it?"

"I think they might've been," I say. Excitement and anger rush into my body, washing away exhaustion and despair. "The shooter made Dominguez think he was part of the team when he came into the house."

"Then we've got them," Cross says with a predatory glint in his eyes. "All we have to do is figure out who was watching the house when Dominguez was shot."

"Time of death would've put it during the shift before ours. Do you remember who we relieved?"

"I honestly couldn't tell you," he says with a shake of his head. "I know that we talked to them, but I didn't recognize either officer."

We hurry to the cruiser, and Cross and I fall into it. He turns the car on and backs out of our parking spot smoothly. "I don't know that Martinez ever told us their names, either."

"But he'll know."

Cross nods. "He'll know."

It's such a little thing, but it's a bridge between what Martinez knows and what we've found. It's enough for us to start putting the pieces together, to bring these people to justice for the harm they've caused. It sings through my blood like triumph, like a predator catching its prey after a long, exhausting hunt. I worry that my grin is feral, too full of teeth, but when I see it returned by Cross, his green eyes glinting in the flashing streetlights we pass, I feel better. There are many reasons why we work well together, but this thrill we feel as we near the end of a hunt is definitely near the top.

I dial Martinez's phone and get his voice mail.

"Meet us at district HQ, Carlos. We've got a tip we need to run by you." I pause, considering. "Bring your list. You know the one I mean."

It's a twenty-minute drive back to HQ. My eyes are gritty with exhaustion, and now that the adrenaline of Dominguez's Reading is wearing off, I find myself yawning every couple of minutes.

"Take a nap," Cross tells me, his eyes on the road.

"I can't." I swallow. "I'm worried I'll keep… seeing

it."

Cross's brow furrows as if he doesn't understand why I would replay that memory again.

"I can't always control it," I admit. "Sometimes, it's just the once, but for intense emotions, the Reading will… linger."

"And this will."

I can taste blood in my mouth, feel it pouring past my fingers.

"For a long fucking time."

"Did my memory linger?" he asks.

My breath catches in my chest. "Christ, Riley, I—"

"I could maybe excuse it," he continues, "you Reading something from me. You're still figuring this stuff out, and I know it kind of… *takes* you when it happens. Maybe it was a mistake. I don't think you'd try to invade my privacy like that. But you didn't tell me about it." He shakes his head. "I don't know how I feel about that, you keeping it from me."

"It happened before any of this"—I gesture between the two of us—"started, and I didn't know how to talk to you about it. By the time I *did*… it was so far in the past, I wasn't sure it mattered anymore."

"Why wouldn't it matter?"

I feel small. "I don't know."

"Are you going to tell me what you saw?"

"It was… I don't…." I swallow hard. "Do you remember when Priya disappeared? When I thought she was gone forever?"

He nods. "When Baker took her. I remember."

"It was that night. When you were watching me sleep."

The car falls silent between us as he absorbs the information. His body tenses when he realizes what it means.

"Ah."

"Yeah, *ah*," I say with a harsh laugh. "How the fuck was I supposed to tell you about that?"

With a groan, he runs his fingers through his hair. "I don't know, Kim, but you could've tried. Jesus."

"It hasn't happened since," I say, slightly panicked. "And I'm sorry."

"I figured since you hid it from me." He glances at me. "You promise it hasn't happened since? That you're telling me everything?"

I don't want to explain to him how visceral the Reading was. That his every thought and feeling had become mine and had tortured me from the moment I Read him until now. He knows enough about Reading to know that it's upsetting, that it's a reliving of a moment. It's enough for him to understand.

"Yes. That's everything."

He sighs. "Okay. I trust you." He reaches for my hand and gives it a tight squeeze. "Try to rest if you can. We're going to be going through those records for a while."

I want to press him for more, for him to forgive me, but I push past it and let myself trust, though it makes my heart race. "You think we're going to get records back fast enough to work on this tonight? Best-case scenario, we get a handful of pictures that I can go through now, and we hit the rest of it in the morning." I glance at the car's clock and sigh. "Records isn't even open this late."

"But the district directory is always available," he says with forced cheer. "There are photos in there of everyone working in the Seventh."

"Dammit," I groan, thinking mournfully of my bed, which I'm probably not going to see for a second night in a row.

CHAPTER ELEVEN

G oing through the directory is mind-numbingly dull. I click through page after page of contact information. Name, phone number, email address, all tucked next to a small low-res photo of the matching officer. The longer I look, the more indistinguishable the faces become. I see skin tone, hair color and length, facial hair or not, male or female, but the fine details disappear beneath my brain's screaming urge to sleep. Words blur and shift, and I blink until they come back into focus. I pray that Martinez will call me, and I can narrow my search to the names on his list, but my phone stays silent as I fight to stay awake.

Through it all, Dominguez's death dances along the edges of my consciousness. As I drift, my eyelids growing heavy, I feel the thud of bullets in my chest and the heat of blood over my hands. My tired mindlessness shifts, and I fight against Dominguez's panic and sudden rushes of adrenaline that have my eyes widening and my breath coming in short bursts.

It's awful.

Meanwhile, Cross is hunched over his keyboard, brow furrowed as he stares at his screen. His notepad is next to him, and small wrinkles gather at the corners of his eyes as he looks between his screen and the paper, transcribing notes from our conversation with Ortega. He's focused, gaze sharp like a honed blade, and as I watch his eyes flick over the words on his screen, his fingers tapping a staccato rhythm on his keyboard, I'm frustrated by his seeming lack of fatigue.

He's always been a dedicated detective, but seeing it in action when I know he has to be as tired as I am is a little overwhelming. The man is a machine when it comes to his work.

"How are you real?" I ask him, the words slipping out before I can stop them.

He looks up at me. "What now?"

"Aren't you tired?"

"Yeah, of course." He sits up and his back cracks loudly. "But we're getting somewhere with this. I'm staying focused on that."

I fight back a yawn. "You might be getting somewhere, but I'm not."

"You haven't found him?"

"Not yet, no." The yawn breaks free. "And there are hundreds of officers in this directory."

He sighs. "Maybe we should call it a night."

I consider putting up a fight, not wanting to give in to my exhaustion, but as I yawn again, I have to agree that it's the best idea. I'm not going to get anything accomplished like this, and don't want to fall asleep at my desk. Instead, I close out of the district directory—I don't bother to note the officer since I'll have to go over everyone again when I come back with fresh eyes in the morning—and shut down my computer. Meanwhile, Cross tidies his desk, putting his paper in neat piles that line up precisely with the edges of the desk. I smile at his fastidiousness and wait for him to finish the nightly ritual.

After he touches the papers, shifting them slightly, he gets the small piles on his desk exactly where he wants them to be, and then he's grabbing his coat from the back of his chair and looking at me with a soft smile.

"C'mon, Phillips," he says. "Let's get out of here."

It's freezing in the parking lot as we both walk to our cars. He stops next to his and stares at me over the roof.

"I'll see you tomorrow?"

I frown. "You don't want to come over?"

"You need to sleep," he says quietly.

"I don't…" I can feel my face flushing. "I don't want to be alone tonight."

"Is the Reading still bothering you?"

I nod and wish he were close enough for me to bury my face in the wide warmth of his chest so I could hide from the fear still clinging to my mind.

"Okay," he says softly. "If you're sure."

"I'm sure."

"Your place or mine?"

I grin, though it feels forced. "My bed's more

comfortable."

"I'll be right behind you."

Getting clumsily into my beat-up Ford, I turn the key in the ignition, blast the heat, and pull out of the lot.

Are you sure you're okay to drive? Priya asks as I yawn before turning onto the street.

Probably, I Send. *I've done this drive a million times and the roads are empty.*

Priya settles in the passenger seat and gives me a long, considering look. *Do you want to talk about it?*

About what? I shiver.

Kim. Her tone is gentle but firm. *You've seen violent death a hundred times. You've never lived it.*

I didn't live it, I Send. *Dominguez did.*

And you lived it through his memories. You've told me what it's like. Don't try to hide from me.

As if I could hide anything from Priya. *It was… I can't find the words. How do you deal with your memories?*

A sharp, stinging pain shoots through our bond, and I wince.

It was a long time ago, she finally says. *I've had time to come to terms with my death. It's still difficult, though, and I won't forget the feeling of it. But it's over, and I'm living what life I have left. With you.*

I nod, then swallow around the lump in my throat. *At least his death was fast. He didn't have time to recognize what was happening.*

That's a bit of comfort, then. Priya sighs. *And it will fade for you, too. Eventually.*

The car falls silent except for the quiet static of tires on pavement. Streetlights flash across the windshield in a bright rhythm that soothes my rough edges. My eyes drift shut, but Priya speaks, shaking me from the tender hands of sleep.

So, Riley knows you Read him.

He does. I glance at her. *Definitely appreciated the support you offered during that extremely embarrassing and emotional moment.*

You needed to handle it on your own, she says soothingly. *If I'd done it for you or told you what to say, you would've made it worse.*

I hate that she's right. *I don't want to mess things up with him, Priya.*

You won't, she says. *As long as you're honest with him.*

I sigh. *You say that like it's something that comes easily to me.*

It wouldn't be worth it if it didn't take some effort.

I don't respond, choosing to sit in my quiet unhappiness instead.

And besides, the two of you are so clearly into each other, it's gross, Priya says sadly. *I thought nothing could be worse than watching the two of you dance around each other, but I was so wrong.*

I laugh, her tone shocking me from my sulk. *You are so full of shit.*

I know, she Sends with a pleased grin. *I love it. You're happy. It's a nice change.*

Yeah.

Her grin grows. *I'd go so far as to say you're giddy.*

I don't do giddy.

That's not what it looks like from here.

I fight the smile tugging at the corner of my lips. Even at my lowest moments, she has a way to draw me out of them. *I'm maybe a little preoccupied*—Priya snorts—*sometimes, but I'm not giddy.*

You tripped over your own feet the other day when he came out of the shower, Kimberly. You are absolutely giddy.

There's a loose floorboard in the living room, I protest.

Bullshit.

I laugh. *Shut up.*

I'm happy you're happy, she says, sincerity making her voice soft. *It's nice.*

It is. I let the smile out. *And maybe I am a little giddy.*

Ah-ha! She points at me, eyes wide. *I knew it!*

Don't gloat, I Send.

I think I deserve to gloat. Didn't I tell you to ask him out?

I scoff. *You did no such thing.*

I said you could do worse.

Of course, I could do worse. I give her a pointed look. *You forget Brandon?*

She laughs. *He would've done you a favor, blowing up your car. This thing is a piece of junk.*

A piece of junk that gets me from point A to point B. I pull off the highway, then turn toward my apartment. *Anyway, Cross is one of the best people I know. He sets the bar high.*

And he likes you for you. Priya smiles. *Trust me, I'm still surprised.*

Doing wonders for my ego here, Priya.

Hush, you know I love you. I wouldn't give you grief if I didn't.

She has a point.

Just promise me that you give Cross a hard time, too, I plead.

Of course. It wouldn't be fun if I didn't bother both of you about it.

I shake my head, smiling, then turn into the parking lot of my apartment building. After parking and turning off my car, I sit inside, waiting for Cross to pull up behind me. The engine ticks quietly as it cools, and I roll my keys around in my hand. They jingle softly, glinting in the glow cast by the building's security lights.

A moment later, Cross's car pulls in and parks next to mine. I step out of my Ford and stand next to the front bumper as Cross gets out and joins me. Though my breath frosts in the air, I feel warmer as he approaches.

"Evening, Detective." His voice is tender, and the small hairs on the back of my neck stand up as it washes over me.

"Evening." I take a step forward and fight the urge to tangle my hands in the lapels of his coat.

He leans down to press a soft kiss to the crown of my head. I feel it all the way to my toes, the brush of his lips crashing over me like a wave. When he pulls back, I try not to sigh. Mouth lifted in a small smile, he takes my hand and laces our fingers together.

"It's late." I take a step toward my building, pulling him with me. "Let's get inside."

His fingers still locked with mine, we trudge up the five flights to my floor. He lets my hand go so I can unlock the door to my apartment, then trails after me as I walk inside.

There's crap everywhere, as usual, and I hear him sigh as he takes in the mess.

"Are you going to let me pick up in here, or no?"

"No," I say and set my keys, gun, and knife on the table by the front door. "You're not my maid."

"No," he says, and though I can tell it pains him, he leaves the mess alone. "I'd get paid if I were."

I fake a laugh and lock the door. Cross's hands fall to my shoulders and gently spin me around to face him. I look up into his green eyes, dark in the muted light of my apartment, and he trails them over my face before leaning in to press a soft kiss to my lips. Breathing in sharply, I let my mouth fall open, and he seals it shut with his. My eyes close. I sink into the sensation, lost for a moment in the soft acceptance of his mouth and body against mine. His fingers slide into the hair at the back of my head, and when he pulls back, he rests his forehead against mine, his eyes shut.

"Stop trying to distract me," he says quietly, and my throat tightens. "Promise me you'll take care of yourself so I don't have to?"

"Of course," I say, though we both know it's a lie. "I'm always careful."

"No, you're not."

He draws me in again, his hands a gentle pressure against the back of my head, which I do nothing to fight against. Warm and soft, his kiss drugs me, draws me in until my eyes slide shut and my mouth falls open. Though desire blazes through me, the kiss stays light, full of some emotion I don't dare name. He pulls away, his hands falling from my hair while the strands cling to his fingers as if they don't want the touch to leave.

"Bed," he says before stepping away. "You need sleep."

We undress quietly, too tired to have more than the most rudimentary of conversations about the day's work. Our elbows bump into each other as we brush our teeth, and I smile around my toothbrush. He meets my eyes in the mirror, and there's a subtle, penetrating expression there that has me looking away.

He leans in to kiss the side of my neck. "Turn off the light before you come to bed."

He leaves the bathroom, and I stare at myself in the mirror. My heart is pounding, my head thick with memory and whatever emotion is crawling its way through my chest. I grip the edge of the sink and fight for balance. Breathing deeply for a few minutes, I find something like solid ground and let my white-knuckled fingers loosen on the porcelain.

Cross is already in bed, the blankets pulled up under his arm while he waits for me. My boots are loud as they hit the ground, and though my back is turned to him as I undress, I feel his eyes like a caress on my skin. I sit on my side of the bed, then slide beneath the blankets. As I lie down, he curls along my back and pulls me tight against his body. His nose buries into the nape of my neck, and it tickles a little when he breathes me in and hums quietly in pleasure.

I let my fingers tangle with his where they rest on my stomach. He squeezes back softly, and I feel his mouth curl into a smile where it rests against my skin.

The lights are off, and my bedroom is cast in dark shadows. There's a slight glow seeping in from the street, but even it seems dimmed by whatever emotion is filling the small room. A heavy lassitude slides over me, trying to draw me into sleep, and as I sink into Second-Sight, I fight it, unwilling to give up the gentle sensation of Cross breathing against my skin.

Green, red, and blue-white lines of power dance through the room, but threaded through them is the quiet golden glow I've come to associate with Cross. It tangles itself around the other colors, blending with them in a random rainbow that calls to me like he does. Eyes heavy, I let them close, the colors still bright in the darkness behind my eyelids. Power twines with power, and as I pull them around us, encircling our bodies with a delicate, protective touch, that golden light gathers around Cross like fireflies trapped in a glass jar. It winks and sparks around him, and though I'm looking away, though my back is pressed against his chest, and his arms are wrapped tight around my middle, there's enough light cast from him and his power that it leaves shadows, even in Second-Sight.

I want to flinch from its heat, but I bask in it instead. I don't understand what's happening to him, what this energy is or why it responds to him and to me the way it does, but it's calming, accepting. It touches the rough edges of my soul and eases them, soothing as it softens me.

I breathe out, and sparks dance around us, small winking lights that remind me of snow, of cinders, and with those stars spiraling around us, I fall asleep.

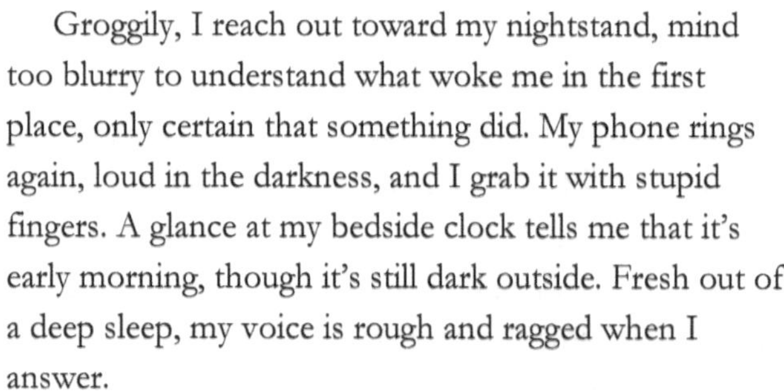

Groggily, I reach out toward my nightstand, mind too blurry to understand what woke me in the first place, only certain that something did. My phone rings again, loud in the darkness, and I grab it with stupid fingers. A glance at my bedside clock tells me that it's early morning, though it's still dark outside. Fresh out of a deep sleep, my voice is rough and ragged when I answer.

"Phillips," I croak.

"It's Lieutenant Walker. Where are you right now?"

I blink the sleep from my eyes, heart pounding as I register the tension in her voice. "I'm at home. Why?"

"We've got a partially decomposed body in an office building. I need detectives on scene ASAP. I'll send you the address. How fast can you be on the road?"

"I thought you were pulling us from everything but the Dominguez case."

"I was," she says, sounding annoyed, "but after the body was reported, someone called Martinez about it."

I rub my eyes, trying to keep up with what she's saying. "That doesn't make any sense."

"That's what I told him. But another detective in Organized Crime had a CI contact her about the building the body was found in, and she says it's owned by the same branch of the Latin Kings that Dominguez was informing on. Martinez wants you and Cross to look into it, see if it's connected."

I turn and look at Cross, whose eyes are half-lidded and red-rimmed. Sometime in the night, he moved from his side to his front, and his arms are wrapped around his pillow instead of me. He gives me a long look, then turns and buries his face in his pillow with a groan. My mouth tugs into a tired grin.

"Give me five minutes to get dressed. I'll head straight over."

"I've been trying to reach Detective Cross, but he's not answering his phone. Get him on the line and have him meet you there."

"Yes, ma'am," I say. "I'll let you know when I arrive on scene."

"There'll be a uniformed officer waiting for you."

"Understood."

And with that, she hangs up. My phone goes quiet, and I let my hand drop before rubbing the corners of my eyes. I hope it's enough to wake me up since I won't have time for coffee before heading to the scene.

Cross groans next to me. "Where do we have to go?" His voice is muffled by the pillow.

I reach over and run my fingers through his hair, letting my hand trail down his neck. Running circles idly over the muscles of his upper back, I indulge in the ability to touch him like this. Quiet and comforting, tender in the darkness before dawn.

"*We* don't have to go anywhere," I say, leaning over to press a kiss to the skin my fingers were touching. "You stay in bed, grab a bit more sleep."

He turns his head to the side to look at me. "I should get up."

His eyes are heavy-lidded and dark. Early-morning stubble clings to his skin like a caress, and I trail my fingers over the line of his jaw, enjoying the rasp against my skin. He pulls his arm from under his pillow to grab my hand and press a kiss to my palm.

"How about you keep looking at me like that instead," I say. "And then you grab another hour of sleep. There's a uniform on scene already. I can secure it on my own."

"If you're sure…" He presses another kiss to my hand, then lets it go. "I'll pay you back next time."

I laugh. "You get to pick up coffee."

"Done."

He shifts his body deeper under the blankets, eyes closed as a soft smile teases the corners of his mouth. I want to kiss it, want to taste his quiet amusement. Instead, I let my eyes trail over his body and the electrifying shape of him in my bed.

A gentle, quiet sense of happiness overwhelms me with its tenderness. It hits me now as I watch his back rise and fall beneath the blankets, the boyish flop of his hair over his forehead, the wrinkles the sheets have pressed into his skin. He's so vulnerable wrapped in white cotton, and with his defenses and guard lowered, I like to pretend he's only ever been that way with me.

Fear grips me, but I shake it off. This is for us. There's no place for worry in this early-morning quiet.

I've never felt like this about someone else before. Never been so equally excited and scared to be with someone in my life. Riley Cross continues to surprise me, daily, and as much as I dislike that sense of chaos, of uncertainty, I thrive on it, too.

As I dress quietly, sliding dark dress pants on and tucking a white blouse into the waistband, I try to breathe through the overwhelming softness in my chest, to not give in to the desire to drop everything and crawl back into bed with him, to drape my body across his and wake him with kisses and gentle touches.

I put my jacket on and linger in the bedroom doorway. Streetlights set his hair glowing, golden brown, and I sigh before heading into the living room. I slip my knife into my boot, grab and holster my gun, and head into the hallway, shutting the door softly behind me. I'll have time to lounge in bed with Cross later. In the meantime, there's a corpse with my name on it.

Chapter Twelve

It's still dark out when I arrive at the crime scene. I hate early-morning calls like these, especially when spring still hasn't fully arrived. A thin sheet of ice clings to the edges of my windshield even though I ran my car's heater full blast during the fifteen-minute drive it took to get here from my apartment. The parking lot is poorly lit, and I vacillate between pulling up beneath one of the few working streetlamps or getting as close to the entrance as I can. Deciding to compromise between the two, I park in the first line of spots along the side of the building and figure the scattered lights on the building will be bright enough for me to see.

The industrial building I'm pulled up to looks ten years out of date and fifteen years out of code. It looms over the nearly empty parking lot surrounding it, my Ford one of the few vehicles parked in its shadow. I climb out, and the sound of my door shutting echoes around the space. The cracked sidewalk I stride down has patches of yellowed grass peeking between the slabs, and the bare trees dotted around the area shift in the sharp breeze as it cuts through my jacket. April in Chicago isn't much better than January, but it's warmer than the day before. There's still a sting to the air, though, especially this early in the morning. I wish I'd brought gloves with me but settle for stuffing my cold fingers into my jacket pockets.

The stucco exterior of the building has been patched in multiple places, the newer material standing out like spotlights. The uniformed officer leaning against the wall near one of the entrances—yellow police tape bright against the dark door—looks like a stain splashed against the pockmarked surface.

The man's older than me by at least a decade and has a few inches on me, too. His hair, though still present, is white and thinning, and his face is lined with deep wrinkles. He holds a lit cigarette between his fingers, and after taking a deep drag, he drops it to the ground. As I approach, he puts it out with a practiced twist of his boot.

He shrugs his uniform jacket tighter around his shoulders. "Detective Phillips?" The question escapes with a cloud of tobacco-scented smoke.

"You've got a body for me?" I ask, flashing my badge.

"Yes, ma'am." He nods toward the building behind him. "It's inside, and—fair warning—it's pretty bad."

"Great," I say, regretting the greasy breakfast I ate on the drive over. "Lead the way…" I trail off.

"Officer Cooper," he says as we walk into the darkened interior of the building. "Jack Cooper."

"Cooper," I repeat. His voice sounds familiar. "Have we worked together before?"

"No, Detective," he says. "I don't think we have."

"Good to meet you, then," I say. "Anything you can tell me about our vic?"

"Not much. Can't even tell if it's a man or a woman, really."

I grimace. If decomp's settled in that much, it can't bode well.

Cooper continues. "The building's only partially occupied right now—it was converted into office space, I guess—so it took a while for anyone to notice. The body's in the boiler room." He shakes his head. "It was pretty obvious where the smell was coming from once they started looking."

"When's the medical examiner arriving?"

"Should be right behind you, I imagine. I called them right after I called you."

Priya, I Send, reaching out for her. *You picking any of that energy up?*

Nothing, she says, appearing next to me as we walk deeper into the bowels of the building. *I don't know whether to be happy about it or not.*

I'll go with relieved, I say, trailing after Cooper as he weaves his way through the labyrinthian corridors of the building. *Do you think it's going away? That's two deaths without any sign of the stuff.*

I don't think we're that lucky.

"How much farther?" I ask, wondering how deep into the basement we're going to have to go, a little surprised that Cooper doesn't appear lost. I can tell we're getting closer to the scene; a rank, familiar scent lingers in the air. Taking in the heavy cinder block walls and the lack of ventilation, it's not surprising that the smell of death is overpowering.

"Not far," he says, gesturing toward the end of the hallway. "It's through those doors."

Up ahead, there's a pair of double doors with a handwritten DO NOT ENTER sign taped to them. I raise an eyebrow.

If it works… Priya says with a shrug. *I don't think Officer Cooper would be able to get a police barrier down here on his own.*

There's always tape. He should have it in his cruiser, I say as Cooper waits for me next to the door. *I'm surprised he didn't call for more backup, either. Or Forensics. They'd be able to set up a cordon as easily as he can.*

"You ready for this?" he asks, reaching into his jacket pocket to pull out a small container of Vicks. He opens it, smears it under his nose, then offers it to me.

Since the smell of decay is already heavy in the air around me, I wave it away. "No, thank you."

He shrugs as he puts it away before snapping on a pair of gloves. "Your funeral."

I put a pair on myself and walk through the doors. Before they swing shut behind us, I'm hit by the overpowering stench of decay. It's a pungent, earthy smell, a mix of wet earth, iron, and blood, overlaid with a sweetness unique to rotting bodies. It sticks to the back of my throat and settles there as I look for the source of the odor.

The room is large, stretching out almost three times its width. Cardboard boxes and wooden pallets are lined up against the wall, along with broken chairs and desks from the office spaces above. There's a filing cabinet with a huge dent in it next to the doors. In the far corner of the room, the boiler rumbles, and the blue light of gas flame glimmers through the large grill on its front. It's hot and cloying in the room and shockingly dark. A few overhead fluorescent lights are the only illumination besides the boiler itself. One flickers on and off, sending the room flashing from light to dark and back again. Between the flashing lights, the wet heat of the room, and the stink, I worry I'll be sick in the middle of a crime scene.

"You weren't kidding," I gasp, fighting down bile. "That's awful."

"They've got some water issues down here, too," he says, nose wrinkled. "It hasn't helped things stay fresh."

Dropping into Second-Sight to better see in the darkness, I take in the corpse lying tucked against a wall toward the back of the room. It's close to the boiler, its back to me, and now that I'm looking at it with Second-Sight, I can tell that the proximity to the roaring heat has sped up decomp. The body's already starting to bloat, and maggots move under the skin that isn't covered by clothing. Liquid seeps from the body, leaving a sluggish stain on the concrete as it flows toward a floor drain.

"Who found it?" I ask, moving closer.

Cooper stays near the door. "Janitor called it in this

morning. Other than him, we're the only people who've been down here."

"And that's the only entrance?" I ask as I gesture back to the double doors.

He nods.

"Okay," I say, circling the body slowly, trying to get a better look. With how it's positioned by the wall and the still-flickering light, it's hard to tell what we're dealing with. "My partner, Detective Cross, is on his way. I want you to watch the entrance of the building until he gets here. Once he arrives, though, I need you to start canvassing. I'm sure there's a building manager or someone here with a similar role. I want their contact information. We need to determine who has access to this room and how a body could've gotten to this state without anyone noticing."

"Yes, Detective," he says, saluting me smartly.

"And we've got to do something about the light in here," I say, gesturing toward the overhead light. "Forensics will have rigs, but if you can find that janitor and get a new bulb or something, that would be great."

He reaches into his jacket and pulls out his cigarettes, tucking one into the corner of his mouth. "I'll get right on that."

"No smoking within the perimeter of a scene," I say, frowning.

He grins, the cigarette bouncing slightly with the movement. "Oh, I know that, Detective. Just getting ready for when we get back outside. Need to get this smell out of my nose, you know?"

I nod. "If you want to head out without me, I'm going to stay and see if I can make sense of what's down here."

He nods, his lighter in his hand as he hesitates by the door. "If you're sure..." he says, brow furrowed.

"Yeah, it'll be fine. I'll be up in a few minutes."

"All right." He flicks his lighter. It rasps quietly, sparks flying from the flint, and with the sharp turn of that wheel, it's like everything shifts into slow motion.

Flames leap from around his hand, moving out in a quickly growing ball of blue fire. They expand in a massive wave, centered around the uniformed officer. As it races toward me, I make out Cooper's shocked face, his wide eyes, and then we're both thrown back by the explosion.

There aren't any windows in the room, so the doors are the only escape for the pressure wave that forms after the fire. They burst open, flames racing into the hallway and throwing Cooper from my sight.

I slam into the far wall, my shoulder and back scraping against the ground as I'm tossed by the explosion, and, as I watch, the ceiling bows up, then comes crashing down. I bring up a shield as the building caves in around me, knocking me to the ground. I curl into a ball, my gloved hands clasped over the vulnerable expanse of my neck and head. The weight of the ceiling hits my shield, stretching my power to its breaking point almost immediately, and I scream, energy burning through me as the shield fights to stay up. Dust whirls, blocking out the flames as I cough in a lungful of the stuff, my eyes and throat burning.

Kim! Priya calls. Eyes whirling white and frantic, she pours her own power into mine, bolstering the shield as it strains. For a second, I think we have it, that we've somehow managed to stop the ceiling from crashing down on me, but then another explosion rocks the building, my power disappears in a rush of flame, and everything goes dark.

Something hits me in the back of the head, hard, and I fall forward, desperately wrapping my hands back around my neck as the ceiling tumbles down around me. Blood streams over my face, warm and sickening. Dust floats, thick and heavy in the air, and I cough and try to blink it out of my eyes. I can feel it coating my skin, thickening where it mixes with my blood.

After the groaning sounds of the concrete above and around me go quiet, I lift my head to look around. Small pieces of rubble and gravel that have landed on my back fall to the floor as I move. There's heat along my side from a wooden pallet that's burning in the cave-like hollow I find myself in. It's the only source of light in the darkness, and looking at it makes my head ache and my vision dance with sparks.

I shift away from the flames, already feeling the temperature rising around me, but as I do, the world lurches. Nausea washes over me, and I vomit up my breakfast. My ears ring as my body is racked with heaves. I try to move from the pile of sick in front of me, but there's nowhere to go. Blood drips onto the concrete, mixing with my vomit, and my stomach heaves again. The small space smells like iron and acid, stone and decay, char and fear.

My headache worsens, a deep-seated pain that sends my thoughts spinning. Flames dance nearby, and for a second, I'm confused about why there's fire so close by. Trying to figure out what's going on, I reach out with my power. The world blinks into Second-Sight, swirling in multihued colors. Pain rockets through me, and I gag before throwing up again.

I taste blood.

Kim, a voice in my mind says, worried and soothing, somehow familiar. *We've got to get you out of here.*

Who are you? I think back, wondering if she'll even hear me. *What happened?*

It's Priya, honey. There are cool fingers at my temple, and I watch as a beautiful Indian woman, ethereal and glowing blue-white, appears before me.

Priya, I say as my mind slips back into clarity. *Fuck, my head…*

I think you have a concussion, she says, eyes worried. *Can you Heal it?*

I'm not a Healer, I say, then shake my head again. It sends pain lancing through me, and I grit my teeth as the world dips and spins. *Wait. Fuck, okay. Let me try.*

After pulling off the nitrile gloves, I draw in power, staring at my hands as it leaps from blue to red to green light, then winks out. I try again, but my head throbs, aches, keens. I close my eyes, heave, spit.

I can't, I Send. *It hurts, Priya.*

Okay, she says reassuringly. *Don't push it. We'll figure this out.*

What happened?

I'm not sure. Some kind of explosion, she says. *You're lucky to be alive.*

I groan and shift away from the burning pallet. It's too hot and sweat drips down my face with the blood.

Where am I?

I can't keep anything straight. Everything hurts. My stomach cramps. My head aches. I look up at the ghostly woman, confusion swirling again.

I need to lie down, I say before shifting from my hands and knees to my side, narrowly avoiding a pile of vomit. *Everything is spinning.*

You need to stay awake, she says as I close my eyes, the darkness welcoming. There's warmth on my face and down my neck. It tickles, and my hand comes away sticky when I brush at it.

Don't you fall asleep on me.

Need to rest a bit.

Kim, don't you dare.

The tone is familiar. I frown, confused.

Mom?

No, Kim, it's Priya, I need you to stay awake, okay? Don't fall asleep. Help is coming, but you've got to stay awa—

Chapter Thirteen

Priya

*O**h shit. Shit, shit, shit.*

Kim is unconscious next to a pile of vomit, buried under what used to be a building. I desperately pour Healing energy down our bond and curse when it does little to stem the flow of blood from her head or bring her back to consciousness. Her suit jacket has protected her for the most part, but there are small cuts over her face and neck. Dust coats everything, turning her skin, hair, and clothes a uniform shade of gray.

If I were still a full Medium, I'd be able to Heal her injuries without trouble. Stitch up her broken skin, soothe the ache in her head, keep her calm while we wait for help. Now that I'm dead, my powers are... *less.* Healing doesn't come easily in Death. The two are antithetical to each other, a dichotomy that I struggled with when I first crossed over. It's gotten easier over the decades, but my Affinity is muted and distant, my abilities limited and weakened. Still, I do what I can, hoping that it'll keep Kim's brain from swelling long enough that help can get to her. Concussions are dangerous, and judging by her nausea, disorientation, and continued unconsciousness, she's got a serious one.

Needing to do something more productive than worry and hover, I look around the small space that she's trapped in, thankful that it appears solid for the time being. There are multiple layers of debris encasing her, steel support beams bent into tangled shapes, wires and cables curled into thick, gnarled knots. Two thick slabs of concrete are protecting her from the rest of the wreckage, but they're also keeping her closed off from easy rescue. Propped against each other, they create a small lean-to that's held off the worst of the debris and saved her life. The bits of burning pallet have me concerned, though, and I cover the flames with a small shield, starving them of oxygen until they gutter out. The wood flickers with embers when I pull back, but I'm no longer worried that Kim will burn to death. At least, not from *this* fire. With the flames gone, the space is completely black, and I switch to Second-Sight.

After giving Kim another careful once-over, I float through the concrete encasing her and take in the rest of the rubble. Lines of green energy outline everything in light, but the chaos around us looks like a tangled mass of bright thread. The swirling confusion only makes it more obvious how precarious Kim's situation is. The damage from the explosion is extensive. As I move higher and higher into the air, I take in the floors of the building, accordioned on top of each other as they collapsed into the basement. Thankfully, the building wasn't that tall, but there are three stories worth of concrete, cinder block, and steel piled on top of my partner. I'm overwhelmed with worry as the magnitude of everything hits me. I hear sirens, but they're muffled by Death and distance.

I sink back into the basement, briefly using my bond with Kim to make sure she's still okay, and fly to where the other officer was thrown by the explosion. He's sprawled in the remains of the hallway we walked down to reach the boiler room, a series of thick, steel support beams bent but holding the crumpled ceiling at bay. The remains of the boiler room doors are crumpled and twisted, broken glass littering the floor. There's burning debris around him, bits and pieces of wood and cardboard that were thrown from the boiler room when it blew. He's passed out, his uniform singed and smoking, but as I run my hands over him, reaching out with thin tendrils of power, I'm relieved to find that his injuries aren't as bad as Kim's. He has a large bump on his head and a few burns that are going to need attention, but he's not in any immediate danger. Nothing is bleeding seriously, and a cursory check tells me that his organs are all undamaged and where they should be. He was lucky. Damned lucky. Ceiling tiles and wires hang down around him, electricity sparking, but he's free of the worst of the damage; as long as nothing else blows up, emergency crews won't have to go far to get him out of the rubble and to safety.

As I watch Officer Cooper helplessly, he rolls from his back onto his side, groaning and coughing. He blinks away dust and rubs his eyes before sitting up.

"What the hell?" he asks, his voice rough. Eyes widening, he takes in the wreckage around him. "Holy shit."

I can tell that he's, unsurprisingly, overwhelmed, but also unaware that there's a way out. Thinking fast, I let power fill my body. As I draw it in, my hair starts to swirl around my head, whipping about in an unseen wind. Energy crackles through me, and as I channel it into my arms and hands, I move in front of Cooper.

Manifesting a physical form is difficult. Death doesn't want us to come back into Life and forcing even a small part of my form through the barrier between the two hurts. But Cooper needs to escape, and I can handle a little pain if it means helping him find a safe way out.

I land in front of Cooper, then pour the energy into my arms and hands. It stings like ice, like flame, but I push through it until I feel the tips of my fingers reaching around on the floor for a piece of burning rubble. Teeth gritted, I grab it and slide it down the hallway, away from the broken remains of the boiler room and toward the open end of the hallway.

I am a ghost, after all. Why not play into the stereotype?

Cooper's head shoots up, following the movement with wide, terrified eyes. When he doesn't move, I do the same with a piece of wood nearby.

"What was that?" he asks before coughing.

I sigh. Mundane people are so bad at this.

Changing my approach, I move behind him and start rattling the doors. When that doesn't get him moving, I keen, my voice low and muffled.

His eyes widen in fear. "What the *fuck*?" he curses, stumbling to his hands and knees. His face is covered in soot and blood from a cut over his eye, but even through the grime, I can tell he's pale. Sweat leaves streaks through the dust, and he starts crawling away from the boiler room.

Getting into it a bit, I shift my focus to my feet. They crunch through broken glass as I walk, and I leave a trail behind me in the mess.

"Oh, hell no."

Officer Cooper crawls forward, pushing wires and small pieces of debris out of his way. I continue to follow him, moaning whenever he slows. Clambering through the dark, he finds the stairs leading to the ground floor and stumbles his way out, cursing the entire way.

I sigh and let the power leave me, my body snapping back into Death. My body glides through metal and concrete as I ease my way to Kim. While I watch, the rubble shifts and falls, knocking into one of the slabs above Kim. The concrete moves almost imperceptibly, but I can feel my heart—which hasn't beat for decades—skip in my chest with fear. Speeding forward, I fly through the concrete to hover protectively over Kim's unconscious body as rocks and debris fall through the wreckage. They ping against the concrete above us, and I pull a shield around our bodies. If the rest of the building were to collapse on top of us, my power won't be able to stop it, but the simple act of protecting my partner makes me feel marginally better. I'm overcome with the urge to keep her safe, to keep her alive. It's staggering, and I know my eyes are swirling white and black, power flowing through me in an overwhelming rush.

The broken structure groans, moves, then settles again, bits of stone skittering to the floor. Relief washes over me as everything goes quiet, stilling. It takes me a minute to calm myself, to fight back the urge to lash out at the world around me. Kim is my tether to Life, and the dark, twisted part of myself that went dormant when we Bonded wants to burst free, to hurt those who would hurt her. Shivering, I push the urge away.

You'd better wake up, I Send, hoping Kim will hear me. *We've got to find a way to get you out of here.*

I watch her breathing, counting her respirations as I try to figure out what to do next. Her eyelids flutter and she groans.

Kim? I rush to her side, letting my hands trail over her body in what I hope is a comforting motion.

"Hurts," she moans, eyes closed tightly in pain. "Where'm I?"

You were caught in an explosion, I Send gently, my heart aching when she winces. *You're safe for now, and help is coming.*

"Who're you?"

It's Priya, I say, chilled to the core. *I'm your partner.*

"Right. Priya." She sighs, her face relaxing as she falls back into unconsciousness.

Dammit.

I brush her hair from her forehead, expending the energy for the motion because I need something physical to tie me to her. Then, I race through the rubble, erupting into the parking lot, our bond stretched as tight as it can go.

The lot is crowded with police cruisers, and as I scan the parking lot, I spot Riley. He's talking to another officer, gesturing toward the building with sharp, jerking movements.

Riley! I shout. Gritting my teeth, I pull the bond between me and Kim to the breaking point. *Over here!*

He looks my way and clenches his jaw when the other officer blocks his way.

What the hell happened? he Sends, his attention clearly split between communicating with me and listening to the officer. *Where's Kim?*

There was an explosion. She's trapped in there, and she's got a serious concussion.

Well, fuck. He nods at the other officer, then pushes his way past.

"Detective!" The uniform tries to stop Riley, but he ignores him and jogs closer to me.

Fire trucks race into the lot, their lights flashing, sirens blaring. As firefighters clamber out of the cab in their gear, Riley slows on the sidewalk next to the collapsed remains of the building, eyes wide and face pale.

How bad is it? he asks, his Sending shaky. *I should've made her wait for me. Dammit.*

She's okay for now, I say, trying to calm him down. *Our bond can't be stretched much farther than this. She's in the basement, in what used to be the boiler room. I know it looks bad, but it could've been much worse.*

You have any idea how it happened?

The other officer—I think his name is Cooper—was playing with his lighter, and then the whole room just… blew up. I think it might've been gas.

Is he okay? Was anyone else inside when the building collapsed?

I haven't checked for anyone else yet. Guilt makes my heart twinge. *But Officer Cooper isn't trapped. He was unconscious initially, and he's got some burns, but he's out now.*

Look for anyone else who might've been caught when the building collapsed, and let Kim know I'm coming for her. I'll go talk to the firefighters, see what we can do to get them inside.

I let him go and head back into the rubble. The strain on my bond with Kim eases as I draw closer, and I settle next to her again in the darkness. Even though she's unconscious, I relay Riley's message and move through the layers of rubble, searching for any other people trapped in the debris. It's hard to see. In Second-Sight, everything is a chaotic series of green lines, all intersecting at various odd angles. With no physical perception of the world around me, I struggle to find hollows and cavities within the destruction. But even with all of the confusion, I don't see anything that looks like a human form in the rubble, and, even better, I don't find any bodies. Officer Cooper had mentioned that the building was only partially occupied, and it's Saturday. Flitting back and forth from Kim's protected recess and the rest of the collapsed structure, my anxiety eases as I don't find anyone else trapped inside. The disaster could've been a lot worse.

Not that it's *great*.

Kim continues to be trapped and has been slipping in and out of consciousness. If the initial explosion was caused by a gas leak, it's likely still leaking into the building. There are fires scattered and spreading throughout the rubble, either from the original explosion or from the snapping electrical wires that wind their way through the remains of the building. Knowing that there could be natural gas leaking into the space doesn't ease the tangle of nerves in my stomach. But, I remind myself, there are emergency crews here. They'll turn off the gas to the property to control the remaining fires. The structural damage, though significant, seems to be isolated to the half of the building that was above the boiler room. And though I can't do much on my own, I have someone I can communicate with, meaning I can guide the rescue efforts.

There's no way I'm going to let anything happen to Kim. As long as she's breathing, I'll protect her with every ounce of my power. I feel my eyes flash white, my hair snapping around my face as energy floods me in a rush. A fierce possessiveness whips through me, and our bond pulses with it. I feel a weak answer from Kim, and she groans, eyelids fluttering.

It'll be okay, I tell myself as I wait for Kim to wake up. *It'll be okay*.

Chapter Fourteen

Kim

The world won't stop spinning. I can't see anything around me—it's pitch black—but I can feel it moving. My head pounds. There's a cool breeze against my forehead. It eases the ache a little. My eyes go distant as I try to see something in the darkness, and I'm met by multihued chaos. Lines of energy whip around me. Green. Blue. Red. Flashes of nothing, then golden light.

Fire?

There was a fire…

Priya? I Send, scared at my disjointed thoughts.

Right here, she says, and the cool touch on my head stills. *How are you feeling?*

What happened?

She sighs, and fear washes over me like a cold breeze.

There was an explosion, she says. From her tone, this isn't the first time she's had to tell me.

Right. How long…?

You've been coming in and out for about twenty minutes, she says. *Fire and police are on the scene.*

Cross? My voice trembles.

Riley's here, and he's doing his damnedest to get you out. She huffs out a quiet laugh. *I think he'd dig you out of here with his bare hands if he had to.*

I grin, and something pulls on my skin.

Blood, maybe.

He's nice, I Send, mind going hazy. *Has pretty eyes.*

Very pretty eyes, Priya says.

Why does she sound worried? I thought she liked Cross. I like Cross.

I close my eyes, shutting out the light. Behind my eyelids, stars and sparks swirl and twist. They make me dizzy, but I keep watching, nausea building. My hands feel far away, and when I tell them to clench, it feels like they belong to someone else when they do.

Don't feel good.

I know, honey. There's a pulse of energy and the sick feeling in my gut eases slightly. *That help?*

Yes, I Send. *Thank you.*

Of course.

Soft, cool touch. Gentle hands. Press of lips against my hair.

Miss you, Mom.

Oh, Kim.

She sounds like she's going to cry.

Wish you didn't hate me.

I don't hate you.

I frown. Her voice is wrong.

Priya?

I'm right here.

Where am I?

God, I can't keep anything straight. I struggle to hold on to my thoughts, but they slip from my grasp, spinning like stars and sparks.

Can't think.

That's the concussion, Priya says softly. *Your brain is trying to protect itself.*

Make it stop.

She sighs. *I don't think I can, sweetheart. I'm doing what I can to help.*

My stomach twists and I gag as nausea rolls through me with unexpected force. Nothing comes out, dry heaves racking my body. Bile and dust coat my tongue. Priya murmurs soothing words through the worst of it, and tears prick my eyes.

I'm in trouble, aren't I?

She laughs, though it sounds forced. *You've always been a fan of pointing out the obvious.*

It's cold.

And it is. I remember heat earlier. Warmth.

Fire.

I shiver. My jacket is wet. Why is my jacket wet?

I touch the floor and my fingers come away dripping. I bring them to my nose, sniff. It's sour and metallic. Water? Vomit?

Why is it wet?

What, honey?

My jacket. It's wet. I'm cold.

There's a soft breath of wind. Silence.

My head pounds.

Nausea. Stars and sparks.

There's water coming in, a voice says. *Only a trickle. If you can shift to the side, there's a dry patch next to you.*

I put my hand on the ground, and something splashes against it. It's thicker and mixed with chunks.

Definitely vomit.

I'm going to need the world's longest shower after this.

Priya laughs, and it sends a lance of pain through my head. *Yes, you will. If you move forward a bit, then lean to your left, there's a bare patch against the concrete.*

I shift, unable to avoid the sick coating the floor, then move forward and to the left. My shoulder brushes something hard, and I reach up to touch it. Rough concrete meets my fingers, and I slide against it, my back pressed into the material as I lie back down.

Can you see anything? I ask as I close my eyes again.

Nothing interesting. Just a ton of concrete, she says. *I can go and see how they're doing outside, talk to Riley?*

No, I Send, throat suddenly choked tight by fear. *Don't leave.*

Soothing touch, soothing words. Cold against my forehead.

I'm not going anywhere.

In the darkness, I can almost forget that I'm buried under the remains of a building. The thought of being alone in this tomb makes me want to scream and beat my fists against the concrete barrier that's simultaneously keeping me safe and keeping me trapped.

I don't remember how it happened. I walked into a building. I spoke with someone. We went downstairs…

Then, nothing.

My head pounds. The vise wrapped around it won't stop tightening.

I wince.

A flash of green.

The pain eases.

I reach for that color again, but the pain comes back, washing away the light in a wave.

Darkness.

Stars.

Sparks.

I'm tired. So tired.

Kim, Priya Sends. *They're going to get you out of here. I promise.*

What happened?

She sighs.

CHAPTER FIFTEEN

RILEY

Any concerns I had while driving to the scene about Martinez's IA investigation or Dominguez's murder are banished in a cloud of smoke and dust that hangs low over the crumpled remains of an office building.

I can't tear my eyes away from the wreckage before me. The concrete walls are listing at awkward, uncertain angles, crumbling and lying on top of each other in layers. Steel and rebar peek out from the broken edges, oxidized brown standing out starkly against the off-white concrete and chipped stucco. The sun is starting to rise and it catches the smoke and dust billowing from the structure. The black cloud above it is cast in shades of red, purple, and gold, looking both ominous and beautiful as it's pulled away by the sharp April wind still whipping through Chicago. I make out crushed pieces of office furniture from under the rubble, and I pray that there weren't people in the part of the structure that collapsed in the aftermath of the explosion. Flames lick out of the building in places, and the frantic, hurried movements of firefighters make my blood freeze.

Staring at the remains of what was an office building only a handful of minutes earlier, I'm overcome by a sense of helpless uncertainty. I want someone to tell me what to do, want to dive into the wreckage and start digging out people—like Kim, but I can't dwell on that thought—from the ruins. I know I'm being impatient. The Chicago Fire Department swarms the area, their black uniforms and helmets glinting in the early-morning light like ants crawling over the ground. There are ambulances standing by, EMS teams waiting with stretchers and metallic blankets for any casualties that might leave the remains of the building. CPD officers have blocked off the streets, set up barrier tape, started talking to witnesses as they work to put the timeline of the accident together.

But as I pace back and forth outside the cordon around the collapsed office building, hands curled into fists and stuffed into my pockets, I want to scream at how slow everything seems to be moving and how helpless I feel in the face of this level of destruction.

I haven't heard from Priya in a few minutes, but I don't want to distract her if she's taking care of Kim. And God, I can't afford to think about that right now. Kim, trapped under three stories of burning concrete and steel, injured, and me, standing out here, useless. A shiver that has nothing to do with the wind tears through me.

I don't want to think about her soft smile as she climbed out of bed. I curled into the warm spot she left in the bed, breathed in the smell of her shampoo and body, and drifted, relaxed and content, back to sleep.

And now, she's trapped, concussed, and curled up beneath the remnants of walls and floors, the building's bones the only thing keeping gravity from bringing its corpse down on top of her.

If this were any other situation, I'd trust Kim to get out of it without issue. But she's not a superhero, powers aside, and being buried under literal tons of rubble is a significantly bigger problem than anything we've run into so far. Even Baker didn't scare me as much as this. I trust Kim with supernatural threats, but this? How the hell does anyone handle *this*?

There are emergency vehicles scattered around the parking lot. Police cruisers, their lights flashing, are near the edges, with fire trucks and ambulances clustered in the center. The ambulance bays are open, all but one of the nervous EMTs standing near the back door of their vehicles and staring at the collapsed building. The odd man out is talking to someone covered in dust, their body wrapped in a silver emergency blanket.

I know it's not Kim. Priya would've told me that she was coming out if that were the case, but my heart is stupid and still hopes it's her. As I draw closer, though, it's clear it isn't. The person's hair is too short, body too stocky. When they cough, the sound is deep and rough, masculine. The EMT stops the man from rising to his feet and murmurs soothing words to him. After a moment, the dust-covered man stills, eyes going soft and unfocused as he stares over the EMT's shoulder toward the building. When I approach, his gaze sharpens, eyes wide as he takes in my suit and the badge hanging around my neck.

His voice is raspy when he speaks. "Detective Cross?"

"Yes."

"Officer Cooper." He coughs again, then spits. "Jesus, I can't get that dust out of my mouth. I'm sorry." His eyes are haunted, regretful. "Your partner's still down there."

I swallow and nod. "I know. Can you tell me what happened?"

"Detective," the EMT warns me softly, trying to stop Cooper from standing again. "We need to treat him for shock."

"I can get treatment and talk," Cooper says, frowning. "Gas explosion, I think. We were in the boiler room, and I was fiddling with my lighter." He drops his head into his shaking hands. "God, this is all my fault."

"You didn't smell gas?"

He drags his palms over his face. "No. The body down there stank to high heaven. I used VapoRub to mask it."

"Probably covered the smell of the gas, too." I want to curse, but I keep my composure, using professionalism to hold back my fear. "Can you tell me anything else about what happened?"

"No, sir. I'm just... I'm sorry," Cooper says before the EMT hushes him again and helps him into the back of the ambulance.

I watch his hunched shoulders, covered by the thermal blanket, start to shake as the EMT closes the ambulance doors behind them. The guy's going to have a lot to think about while the rescue operations get moving. I hope it doesn't weigh on him too heavily, but judging by the defeated slump of his back and the way his voice trembled when he spoke, I don't think that'll be the case.

Turning back to the building, I move close enough to Send to Priya. *I just met Cooper. He's shaken but doesn't look too bad,* I say, reaching out with the new ability I'm still learning to use. *How's Kim?*

The answering silence makes my blood freeze. *Priya?*

She's getting more confused, Priya finally responds. *I'm worried, Riley.*

I curse. *Do what you can for her, okay? Procedure for these situations is to not let anyone in until the fire department is sure it's safe, and I don't know how long that's going to be.*

"Detective," a voice says, and it breaks me from my Sending. I turn to find a firefighter waiting, expression serious. "The structural engineer has arrived, and Command wants to discuss next steps."

I nod, then follow him toward the command center that's quickly formed. It's not much—a white plastic folding table surrounded by men and women in various uniforms—but it's a place to gather. I'm sure it'll turn into something more impressive during the next couple of hours, but for now, it's a crowded place for worried faces to look back at each other and plan.

I approach and wedge myself into the circle of uniforms. A short woman in a black helmet and heavy black jacket with strips of reflective tape looks up at me. She's got dark, curling hair pulled into a low ponytail and eyes such a deep shade of brown, they almost seem black. Dust from the scene has settled on her face, standing out against the brown of her skin in gray streaks. There are blueprints spread out before her, her hands calm and confident as they smooth the plans onto the table.

"Detective Cross," I say, nodding instead of offering my hand.

"Lieutenant Emily Reddick." She looks back down at the blueprint. "Let me get you up to speed. We've got a partial collapse of the structure, mainly in this area." Her finger traces over about two-thirds of the building. "The far end seems to be intact and still safe to enter, but this whole section is compromised. Multiple load-bearing structures appear to be weakened or gone. We've got fires here"—her fingers move over the paper—"here, and here. We don't know how many people are trapped inside, so our first concern is getting those fires under control, then shoring up the structures so Urban Search and Rescue can get in safely. We know that a good portion of the building was unoccupied, so we're thankfully not expecting many victims. ComEd is shutting off power to the building, and People's has already cut off the gas flow. We're going to start spraying water soon, though we're going to try to keep that to the active fires as much as possible in case there's anyone trapped inside."

"My partner is in the basement," I say. "In the boiler room."

"You know that for a fact?"

"Yes," I say with a swallow. "She's a Medium. I've been talking to her Bonded ghost."

Reddick's eyebrow lifts hopefully. "Shaker?"

"No. Burner."

"Of course, we're not that lucky." She curses. "That would've been helpful as hell. I think USAR is trying to find one to bring to the scene, but you know how long that can take."

I don't, but I nod anyway.

She flips the top three sheets of paper back with practiced ease, then points to one of the rooms delineated in careful, straight lines. "Well, if she's down there, it's going to take some time to get her out. That whole section is the hot zone, and we're not sending anyone in until we get the rest of the building shored up." Eyes rising to land on the building behind me, she frowns. "That's gonna take a lot of work."

"So, what, we just leave her there?"

Reddick doesn't look happy with my question, but her words are gentle when she speaks. "For now, yes. I understand your concern, Detective, I really do, but we're going to focus on the surface victims and walking wounded first. We need to clear the scene of as many people as possible before we start moving around in there. You see what we're dealing with. We can expect secondary collapses if we're not careful, and I'm not putting any rescue teams in there unless we're *damned* careful about it."

She sighs as my expression tightens. "If you're in contact with her, keep up the conversation. Do what you can to help her stay calm. See if she can provide us with any information about where she is or how we can get her out. I heard we had someone else exit the scene from that area?"

I nod again. "Yeah, another officer."

"We'll talk to him, see what he can tell us about the state of the building. Maybe he can help us target our rescue efforts. But"—she tilts her head, looking at me from under the brim of her helmet—"you need to let me do my job."

"Understood." I'm not happy with her answer, but I understand it.

"Okay," Reddick says. "Moving on."

I half listen to her go over the pre-rescue operations, outlining the first steps and what she expects the resources on scene to do and take responsibility for. When she finishes, she dismisses the people clustered around her. Everyone walks off with a purpose, but I'm lost. Other officers are keeping civilians out of the area, and aside from joining them, there's not much I can do besides wait.

I reach out for Priya again, questing for her presence and a way to feel like I'm not standing here with my thumb up my ass. *What's going on down there?*

She sighs. *Nothing new, I'm afraid. She keeps going in and out of unconsciousness, which concerns me. With a concussion this severe, there's a big risk that her brain will start swelling, and if that happens, there's not a whole lot we can do outside of a medical setting.*

Shit.

Yeah. There's also hypothermia to consider. It's not exactly balmy out right now, and there's some standing water where she's stuck. All the concrete isn't going to help things, either. I hope you have some good news for me.

Yes and no, I hedge. *The good news is that the gas has been shut off, and ComEd is working on turning off the power. Bad news, CFD's got a couple of fires to fight, the structural damage is extensive, and Kim's in the middle of the worst of it. It's going to be a while before they let Search and Rescue in.*

So, even though I can tell you exactly where Kim is, she's stuck for the time being.

And any other people trapped inside, yeah.

Priya curses. *I'll keep doing what I can to help her, and I'll search for more victims to be on the safe side. I didn't see anyone else earlier, but I could've missed something. It's hard to tell what's what in here.*

She pauses, and I grow concerned.

I don't like how disoriented she is or her inability to stay conscious. That's a bad sign when it comes to traumatic brain injuries. We're going to have to get her out of here, preferably as soon as possible.

Trust me, Priya, I say through my anxiety, *I want her out of there as much as you do.*

I know. I'll talk to you soon.

Keep her safe for me. For us.

She doesn't reply, and I storm away from the building. I haven't felt so useless in my life. Desperate for something to do, I turn back toward Command and pray that they have something to keep me busy.

Anything to stop me from losing my mind with worry.

CHAPTER SIXTEEN

RILEY

Time drags on as USAR and CFD plan how to safely remove the rubble. Not that they've started moving it, but there's been plenty of planning. Wooden structures spring up around the building, shoring up the unsteady remains of walls before teams in black and navy blue gather together, talk, and continue to do nothing.

At last, Lieutenant Reddick not-so-subtly chases me off to help oversee the perimeter with the uniformed CPD officers on scene. I don't blame her. My anxious hovering isn't helping anyway, but as I continue to struggle with the lack of anything *useful* to do, I hate the distance between me and the center of everything, and from Kim.

As I wander back and forth along the cordon, keeping people from crowding in too close, a flash of yellow catches my eye. I squint, then see a familiar, scowling face looking at me from the edges of the crowd. He's wearing a black beanie pulled low over his eyes. His puffy, yellow jacket is zipped up tight this time, and he looks like he's lost in it.

Our eyes meet, and his widen before he turns and starts walking quickly away.

What the hell is Herrera doing here?

A combination of instinct and a need to do something has me shadowing him from the other side of the cordon. He catches my movement and speeds up. I wave at another officer, getting her attention. "Kid in the yellow coat," I shout, pointing toward Herrera as he starts to disappear into the gathered crowd. "Don't let him get away!"

The office building is located on the South Side— Kim and I wouldn't have been called to the scene otherwise—but it's nowhere near the street corner we found Herrera on the day before. Based on the distance, I can't think of a good reason for him to be here. It's too much of a coincidence to think he happened to be walking by and saw the building collapse. He's here for a reason, though I don't have any idea what it might be.

Ducking past the wooden police barriers that make up the cordon, I shove my way through the heavy crowd that has gathered around the scene. There's only minimal space between the gawkers, and as I try to cut through to the empty street right past them, the crowd seems to draw closer, cutting me off. People yell out as I lurch through the swarm, refusing to move even as I tell them to.

"Chicago Police!" I grab at the badge around my neck, waving it as another man refuses to move. "Get out of the way!"

The crowd finally parts, and I start running after Herrera, who's almost disappeared around the corner. I curse and break into a sprint, my leg muscles burning. April in Chicago is cold and wet, and this morning is no different. The air rushing into my lungs stings, a sharp ache that worsens with each panting inhale. Sweat beads beneath my jacket and runs down my back. My steps are loud as my feet slap against the ground, my strides eating up the sidewalk beneath me as I draw closer to Herrera.

He glances over his shoulder, his eyes widening as he takes me in, barreling after him.

"Oh shit," he says loud enough for me to hear over the pounding in my ears, and then he's running faster, his arms pistoning back and forth as he tries to get away.

No way in hell am I letting that happen.

I grit my teeth, put my head down, and race forward. He's just out of my reach, so I lunge for him, my arms stretched out and my hands like claws as they scramble for a grip on his jacket. The smooth synthetic fabric slips beneath my fingertips, but I manage to get a handful of his jacket before I lose my balance and take both of us to the ground.

We crash into the unforgiving concrete sidewalk, and I hear fabric tear as we slide across the ground. Herrera is cursing a blue streak in a mix of English and Spanish, struggling and trying to break free of my grip. I grapple with him, wrapping my arms around his chest and pinning him to the ground.

"The fuck is wrong with you?" he shouts, twisting his body to shake me from my position against his back. "I wasn't doing anything!"

"Shut up!" I pant as I try to catch my breath. "And stop fucking moving!"

"No way in hell, *pendejo*!"

I see red but grit my teeth against the anger. After a moment, I hear more footsteps behind us, and as I turn my head to the side, I make out the other officer I yelled to earlier.

"Cuffs!" I shout, and she hurries over, looking confused and a little scared, and pulls a pair from her duty belt. I manage to wrestle Herrera's arms around his back, the kid cussing and jerking in my grasp the entire time, and she puts the cuffs on him.

"Fuck you," he spits as I pull him to his feet. "You arresting me? I didn't do nothing!"

"You're the idiot who ran," I say, pushing him in front of me. "What the fuck are you doing here?"

"I wasn't *doing* anything!"

He sounds panicked, and now that I'm not chasing after the kid, adrenaline fading from my system, I'm starting to realize that I've chased down and cuffed an unarmed kid who, as far as I know, was minding his own business. What a fucking mess. I shut my eyes but keep moving him down the sidewalk and back toward the collapsed building. Cold air whips through a long rip in my jacket, and I shiver as the sweat on my skin cools and dries.

As we draw closer to the fallen structure, he stops struggling. I move him past the cordon, the gathered crowd watching us with interest, and direct him toward my cruiser.

"Jesus Christ," he says quietly. "What the fuck happened?"

"Gas explosion," I say before opening the back door to my car and pushing him inside. I climb into the front passenger seat, slam the door shut and turn to look at him.

His arms are still cuffed behind him, and he's sitting sideways on the back seat. Mouth slightly open and eyes wide, he stares out the opposite window at the remains of the building.

"That shit was three stories," he says, stunned. "How fucking big was the explosion?"

"Big enough." I snap out the words, and he looks back at me with a hint of fear and defiance in his eyes. "Now, tell me what you were doing here."

"I'm not telling you anything, asshole." He looks around the car, eyes suddenly sparking with mischief. "But if you bring your sexy partner over here, I'll tell her whatever she wants to hear."

I count down from ten and remind myself that first-degree murder means twenty to life.

"She was in the fucking building," I grit out, temper barely held in check. "Now, talk!"

Herrera's eyes widen. "Oh shit." He glances back at the building, then at me with a wince. "I'm sorry… I mean, I didn't know her or anything, but that… that sucks, dude."

When I don't say anything, he looks away, visibly uncomfortable. After a moment, he starts speaking.

"I… I do some business around here. Nothing you'd give a shit about, but I'm not gonna give you details or anything. It's just drops, usually. Nothing today," he says, glancing back up at me as if I'll bust him for some stupid drug shit. "I'm not carrying."

"Of course, you aren't," I say with a sigh. "You just leave shit in the parking lot, or what?"

He shakes his head. "No, there's a guy…" He trails off. "Guess it doesn't matter now since it's all fucking gone."

"How long have you been working out of this place?" I ask.

"Couple of months. Since the summer, at least."

I frown. "And you're the only person making drops here?"

"No," he says with a shake of his head. "Couple other guys do it, too. Drop-offs and pickups. Shit, this is going to fuck things up."

"Why are the Latin Kings working out of an office building?" I ask, but he looks at me like I'm the idiot here.

"Why would I know that?" He laughs. "Shit, *cabrón*, you're lucky they let me know my name."

I most definitely do not like this kid. After a long moment, he shifts in his seat and tries to roll his shoulders.

"So, are you gonna arrest me, or what? I'm not carrying, I swear."

As much as I'd like to, I've got nothing on the kid, and Lieutenant Walker isn't going to give two shits if I catch a kid on a misdemeanor drug charge. I eye him carefully, and when he sits up a little straighter, his spine stiffening with defiance, I know I'm not going to get anything else out of him today. With a frown, I shake my head. "No."

I get out of the car, then let him out of the back seat. He shimmies his way to the door and shoots me a look that's full of malice and vindication as he stands. I lead him to the edge of the cordon, as far away from the crowd as I can get him, then undo his cuffs. He rubs his wrists and opens his mouth to speak, the glint in his eyes telling me he's about to spout off with some smart-mouthed comment. But his eyes dart behind me to the ruins, and whatever words he was about to let loose fall dead between us.

"Sorry about your partner," he says instead. It's quiet, almost mumbled, but I nod, throat tight. "She seemed nice, I guess. For a cop."

"She's not dead," I say softly. "We're going to get her out."

An eyebrow raises. "Of course, you are, man." He rubs his wrists again and looks away. "Of course, you are."

He takes a step back, then another before turning his back to me and wandering into the crowd, his yellow jacket disappearing in the sea of gathered bodies.

I turn my back on him and the crowd, cursing, and walk toward the building. Why the hell would the Latin Kings have a base of operations in an office building? I could understand a flophouse or a small business, but this place was three stories, multiple offices. A hundred people in and out every weekday. It's far from a low-profile location and certainly not a way to avoid notice. Kids like Herrera would stand out like a sore thumb. I reach for my phone and dial Martinez.

"Hey," he says, answering almost immediately. "I just saw you on the news. What the fuck happened?"

"Gas explosion," I say for what feels like the hundredth time this morning.

"Yeah, I saw. I meant what the fuck are you still doing there?"

I frown, though he can't see it. "Kim and I were called to the scene. Body in the basement. But she got here before I did, and…"

"Yeah, I know," Martinez interrupts. "I asked Walker to send you guys."

"Why would you want us here?"

"The building is owned by the Latin Kings, same group that Dominguez was informing on. Didn't Walker tell you about this before you left?"

I rub at the space between my eyes, fighting off a headache. "She called Kim about it, not me."

"And Phillips didn't say anything about it?"

"Didn't have a chance." I swallow. "Kim was inside

when the explosion happened. She's trapped."

"Well, shit." Martinez sighs. "How're you holding up?"

"I've been better. It's slow going, but CFD and USAR are starting to dig her out. Anyway, that's not why I called you. I found one of Dominguez's known associates hanging out nearby."

"Riley," he says, sounding confused, "why are you working the Dominguez murder right now?"

"I need to do something, Carlos." The words slip through my gritted teeth. "I was getting in the way."

"Okay," he says soothingly. "Okay, I get it. Tell me what you got from the guy."

"His name's Herrera. We tried talking to him yesterday"—holy shit, was it only yesterday?—"and couldn't get him to say a damn thing. But that wasn't the case today."

"So, what'd he tell you?"

"He's been making drops here, and some other guys he knows were doing pickups. Guess it makes sense that he was hanging around here if the Latin Kings own the place."

"I'll look into the drops, see if they're connected at all," he says. "I got some interesting news from Forensics this morning, too. That broken window on the back door?"

"Yeah?"

"It was broken from the outside," he says, "which is what we expected. But the glass on the floor wasn't broken a second time."

I frown. "So, when the guy got inside, he didn't walk through it."

"Exactly."

"I mean, he didn't leave any prints, either. Our guy could have been careful."

Martinez hums through the line, his tone considering. "Maybe. It feels like more than that, though. I got a voice mail from Phillips last night, too. You know what that was about?"

I groan. "Yes, but it's worthless until we get her out of that rubble. She was able to get something off of Dominguez's body last night."

"With her ghost powers and shit?"

"Yeah," I sigh, "with her ghost powers. She saw the guy who shot him."

Martinez swears. "What's the timeline for getting her out of there?"

I give him a quick rundown of the scene, what the plan is, and how much longer we're expected to wait.

"You focus on getting Phillips out of that mess," he tells me after a long moment. "She's good people, and we need what she knows."

"Yeah." I rub the bridge of my nose. "Call me if you hear anything else from Forensics or the ME. I need to go."

"Be safe, man," he says.

"Will do."

I hang up. My throat tightens as anxiety rushes

through me. I clench my hands into fists to keep them from shaking. Reaching out, I search for Priya, letting my mind seek out her familiar, comforting touch. I know she and I talked not that long ago, but I need to know how Kim's doing. I know her condition isn't likely to have changed, but I can't stop myself from reaching out. I poke at it like an aching tooth, knowing that it'll only bring pain but unable to stop myself.

I feel Priya on the edge of my mind and grab for her. There's that sense of connection, of hearing without sound as I start to Send.

Priya, how's Kim?

Cross?

I frown. Her voice sounds different.

Priya?

I'm right here, she Sends, appearing next to the rubble a moment later. *Are you okay? You sound weird.*

Yeah, I'm fine. How's Kim?

She's okay, she says, though she won't meet my eyes when she says it. *How are things going out here?*

I look toward where USAR has started removing rubble. A line of men and women in hard hats and respirators are passing pieces of broken cinder blocks and concrete from the base of the building toward a slowly growing pile in the parking lot. Firefighters are wrapping up lengths of hose and packing them back up in their trucks, talking quietly among themselves as some peel off to join the human chain. The dust and smoke that was rising from the ruins has dissipated, and

I let out a relieved breath once I realize that the major fires must be extinguished at long last.

Looks like things are moving, I Send. *Finally.*

That's good. How long do you think it'll be?

I take in the still-massive pile of wreckage, the slow movement of debris, and the pounding of my heart in my chest.

Long enough. I'm going to help.

Take care of yourself, she warns. *Kim's going to need you once we get her out of there.*

I know, but I need to stay busy until then. I won't overdo it, I promise.

She smiles at me, though it's muted with worry. *I can't take care of both of you. I don't have that kind of time.*

I laugh, like I know she wants me to. *Keep an eye on her, okay?*

Of course. Always.

She disappears, her presence in my mind fading as quickly as she fades from Second-Sight. I approach the firefighter in charge of the human chain, rolling up my sleeves as I walk.

"How can I help?" I ask.

He points me toward a pile of respirators and hard hats. "Get some PPE on and join the line. Keep the rubble moving. Take breaks when you need them. We're going to be here for a while."

I nod, then grab supplies before losing myself in the physical monotony of the human chain, relieved to finally be doing something useful.

CHAPTER SEVENTEEN

KIM

Black.

Pain.

I blink, trying to chase it away.

Cool fingers on my brow.

Kim. You've got to wake up, honey.

Recognition. *Priya?*

I'm right here.

Sudden, rushing relief that's cut off too soon. I groan and press a hand to my head, the ache lessened, though my fingers come away sticky with drying blood and dust.

Did you Heal me? I Send. It still hurts, but it's not the same shooting pain as before.

A little, Priya says. She sounds hesitant, which is odd, but I brush my worry aside as she continues speaking. *I've been helping as much as I can. How are you feeling?*

It still hurts to use my powers. Even Sending. And I keep getting nauseous.

You're concussed.

Oh, really? I didn't know. I feel her glaring at me. *Sorry. I just… I feel awful.*

I know, honey. Don't push yourself too much. You need to save your energy.

What I need is to get out of here. I reach forward and the palm of my hand smacks into hard, cold concrete. Feeling around, I try to gauge how much space I have, but it's hard to tell.

I know I've woken up before. There's a vague sense of memory, a series of flashing images that I can't put together into a cohesive whole. I know time has passed. I know that work is being done to help free me. The specifics, though, are missing. Risking the pain and needing to know more, I drop into Second-Sight. It sends my stomach twisting, and I fight against the urge to vomit. My mouth tastes like sour metal as I scan the space as quickly as possible.

There are two pieces of thick concrete directly above me, one leaning on the other. Together, they've formed a slight lean-to structure that's kept the rest of the debris from killing me. Scree covers the ends of the small space: rocks, pieces of broken and charred wood, and gravel tumbled into a jumbled barrier that prevents me from seeing anything else. I shuffle to the middle of the space, wincing as my knees drag through gravel and vomit, and reach my arms out, trying to determine the size of the space. I can't extend them fully, my fingers brushing concrete before my elbows can unfold. The space is longer than it is wide, though not by much. I'm able to rise to my hands and knees in the very center but lifting upward even slightly more than that brings my back into contact with the pointed "roof" above me.

If I had to guess, the rectangular space I'm in is about four feet long and three feet wide, though the leaning slabs lessen my effective space to two, maybe two-and-a-half feet since the angled concrete causes the very edges to be too small for me to make any use of the space there.

As soon as I drop from Second-Sight, my head pounds and my stomach turns.

Bile, thick and burning in my throat, followed by pain.

So much *pain*.

I power through it, holding back nausea with gritted teeth and tightly shut eyes. Slowly, it eases, fades, until I can open my mouth for a gulping, dust-choked breath. My body shakes with the effort, exhaustion weighing as heavy on me as the concrete wreckage trapping me here.

I can't see them, but my hands are shaking.

I shift onto my left side. The concrete is ice cold and quickly leeching warmth from my body. My jacket and clothes are soaked through all along my side, too, clinging to my body. I run my fingers over the ground, and they come away cold and wet.

Water's still leaking in, I Send, vaguely remembering Priya saying something about it earlier. *You said it was dry over here.*

It's a relative term, Priya says, sounding apologetic. *The flow got stronger once they started fighting the fires above you.*

I'm buried under a fire?

Maybe.

Priya.

She lets out a slow breath. *You were. They've got it under control now, but the explosion started a lot of them. There was only one near you, thankfully.*

This sucks.

I know, honey. Let's focus on your head first. How's the pain?

If I'm not doing anything, manageable.

But using your powers makes it worse.

Yes.

She doesn't say anything for a long moment, and at first, I think she's left. I reach for her along our bond, wincing, and feel her answering comfort.

I'm thinking, she Sends. *Give me a moment.*

I wait in the silence. My heart pounds in my ears, labored breaths whistling against my chapped lips as I exhale. The building moans, shifts. Water falls in a steady, continual drip. I smell dust and blood and a hint of rot, the sickly-sweet odor of vomit. My mouth is rancid, and the back of my throat is sore and tight from throwing up. My eyes are shut against the blackness, and white dots and lines dance behind my eyelids, my brain creating light where there is none. The shapes linger when I open my eyes, and I see something move in the endless darkness, though I know there's nothing there—only concrete an arm's length away.

At last, Priya speaks. *I want you to try something if you think you can.*

Will it make me feel better?

Maybe, she says unconvincingly. *It could make it worse.*

Groaning, I press the heels of my hands to my eyes. The whole situation feels hopeless. I'm fighting against panic, but it's coming hard and fast as my mind shifts and clears. There's nothing I can do. I'm trapped. I'm weak and lost and hurt. Buried under tons of rock and twisted metal. Soaked and cold. Sick and scared.

I'm not going to cry.

Okay, I Send shakily as tears prick the corners of my eyes.

Priya shushes me, murmurs quiet, comforting words that help soothe my racing heart. When my breath no longer stutters from my chest, she starts to speak.

I can't help you as much as you need. My powers aren't strong enough, and as much as I wish I could Heal that hit to your head, I can't. But you can.

Priya, I—

I told you to listen. Her voice is sharp. It's the first time I've heard her sound scared. *You* are *a Healer. Just like you're a Burner and a Reader. I know it's new, and I know you haven't had much need to practice using those powers, but you need to use them now. I never Mentored another Medium, but I taught at the hospital, and I was a Healer. We'll make this work.*

Okay, I say, surprised by the intensity and fear in her voice. *What do I do?*

Relief sings down our bond, followed quickly by a

pulse of love and determination. *I want you to reach for your Healing, bring it to the forefront. If it starts to hurt, stop pushing. I'm worried that using your powers may worsen your symptoms, including any intracranial swelling. Once you have it, though, let me know.*

I nod and close my eyes. It's as dark behind my lids as it was with them open, but the simple motion, the familiarity of it, helps calm and center me. Inhaling slowly, rock-flavored air flows over my tongue, through my throat, and into my lungs. I hold it, then release it on an even exhale.

I dip into Second-Sight. Colors twist around me, bright lines of power snapping and swirling in odd, tangled masses. Chaotic and beautiful, it makes my head pound. I pull back, letting the light fade until it's only a hint of power. Then, I focus. Blue-white light flashes, familiar but unwanted now. Red, then green, and I drive toward that color. The color of fresh grass, of leaves budding on trees, of growth and life. It flows to the front, the red and blue dimming and fading into the background until I'm surrounded by swirling lines of green, green, *green*.

I've got it. My voice is hushed. Throat tight as I fight for control, I reach for the power. *Now what?*

Let it build in your body, Priya says. *It will want to go to where you're injured. It's drawn to damage. But if you don't keep it under control, it will go after anything and everything it can find and leave you drained. It can kill you. So be* careful, *Kim. Direct it. Command it. You're the Medium. It's just the power.*

I swallow and slowly open myself to it.

Power comes rushing into my body like someone returning home after a long absence. It's joy, relief, a warm welcome. Tender and questing, it wants to buck off my tenuous control and make everything all right again, and, God help me, I want to let it. It whispers to me that it will take care of me, take my pain away. Everything will be healed as long as I let it go. Just let go, give in, give up.

Priya, I groan. *It's too much. I can't...*

Power screams through our bond, and the grass-green energy trying to take me over grows thorns, fighting against Priya's sudden grasp around its neck. It twists and tangles its way through my body, digging into my veins and arteries, wrapping tight around my heart. I want to scream, but there are roots growing in my throat, choking me

No. Priya's voice echoes in my mind, fierce and commanding. *She's* mine.

Two forces, pulling me apart, tearing into me with fingers like bones, tendrils like razor wire. I open my mouth to scream, and light bursts from my mouth.

Green.

Then black.

I curl into myself, panting. When I spit, I taste dirt and leaves.

Jesus fucking Christ, I Send. *What the fuck.*

Sorry. Priya settles next to me, and I shiver in the cold. *I warned you.*

You didn't tell me I'd like it.

Silence. A cold touch on my hair. A breeze against my face like a forgotten kiss.

Are you ready to try again?

I swallow. Grass taints my tongue. Fear tangles in my chest like weeds, like roots.

Yeah.

I tell myself that I know what's coming this time, that I'm prepared for it, but as I let the Healing energy flow into my body, I'm overcome by the desire to let it free, to let it wash away all of my pains. Teeth gritted, I fight. I fight against it harder than anything else I've fought in my life, leashing it with a strength I didn't realize I possessed. It fights me with briar and brambles, thistle and thorns. Tears through me as I draw it toward my aching head. But as I direct the energy to the laceration, it calms. As soon as I loosen my grip, it erupts in a wave of green. It pours into the wound, winding its way around the tissues and capillaries, stitching it together with curling vines of power. I'm washed away on soft, fresh grass, the smell of wet earth and spring heavy in my nose and throat. Cool water on a parched throat. Spring warmth after a long, cold winter. Rest. Peace.

Kim! Priya shouts, and her power comes racing into my mind, leashing the Healing energy as it knits my skin back together. *Hold it back! It's too much, too fast.*

I don't want to. I want to sleep. Lay down my worries and burdens and be washed away on this cool, easy current. But with Priya's voice screaming in my ear and distant, distracted fear pounding in my chest, I cut the power flowing through me. It shudders, fighting the command, but then it stops, and as I gasp, my body collapses against the ground. I taste dust and water.

Grass and blood.

And then exhaustion rips through me like a tide. My body shakes as it breaks out into a cold sweat. Everything hurts, a low throbbing ache that will only go away with sleep. Even though I'm uncomfortable, even though the ground is hard and wet, even though it's pitch black around me and I'm trapped, I slip easily into unconsciousness, Priya's voice fading into the darkness with me.

Chapter Eighteen

Riley

Removing debris is backbreaking labor, but it keeps my idle hands busy. Eventually, the firefighter leading the chain is replaced by a man in a navy blue jumpsuit with reflective tape looped around his arms and chest. He directs everything with practiced ease. His eyes are shaded by his hard hat, but his voice is loud enough to hear even from far away.

My hands are freezing and starting to chafe from the broken bits of concrete that are passed to me, but I ignore the slight pain until there's a break in the line and I can put on my gloves. They're black leather and stop the stone from stealing the heat from my hands. I wonder how Kim's doing, if she's starting to get cold, and I push the thought away violently, losing myself to the back and forth of removing rubble.

After twenty minutes, there's a layer of sweat between my dress shirt and my jacket, and my hands are slick inside my gloves. I pant with exertion, and the moisture of my breath clings to my face inside the respirator. I'm either unwilling or unable to step out of the line to rest. Though they ache, I force my muscles to keep moving stone after stone, block after block, my mind empty of thought.

My phone rings in my pocket, the sound shaking me from my near-fugue state. I finally stumble away, hands shaking as I take my gloves and respirator off and let someone else fill in the empty space in the line.

When I pull out my phone and see Andrea Banks's name on the screen, though, I decline the call and move back toward my abandoned station. A few seconds later, the phone rings again.

Annoyed, I pick up almost immediately. "What is it, Andrea? I can't talk right now."

"What the hell happened? I saw you on WGN."

"Fuck." I'm tired, and the curse slips out before I can stop it. "Of course, you did."

"Why are you at the site of an explosion? Aren't you Homicide?"

"I can't talk to you right now," I force out. "I'm a little busy at the moment."

"Where's Kim?" Fear clouds her voice, and guilt mixes with my urge to hang up on her. "Are you okay?"

"No." I exhale, and it shakes its way from me, leaving my chest empty and hollow. "No, I'm not. And Kim…" My voice breaks for the first time today. "Kim's inside."

"Oh shit." There's a long pause. The city speaks over her ragged breaths, its voice a shrill mix of car horns and sirens. "Is she…"

"She's alive," I say, trying to calm the panic I hear building in her voice and to reassure myself. "She's trapped, but Kim's still alive."

"Thank God for that. Can you tell me anything?"

"Off the record?" I ask, trying to break the tension that lies taut between us.

She laughs. "And I thought Kim was the asshole…"

"CFD's working on getting people out and stabilizing the worst-hit areas. Urban Search and Rescue are removing debris, and they're bringing in a Shaker from Atlanta. He's on a plane now, should be arriving later this afternoon."

"How soon can they get Kim out?"

"No idea," I say. I'm proud that my voice doesn't shake anymore, but the words make a tight ball of fear clench in my chest. "It's all dependent on how long the shoring and debris removal take."

"I'm heading your way. I can help."

"You're not going to be allowed through the cordon, Andrea." If she were a full Medium, then maybe, but since she's only Sighted—and a reporter to boot—there's no way CFD is going to let her in. I try to soften the blow anyway. "If you're not a trained first responder, the fire department won't let you through."

"Well, then, what can I do to help?" Her frustration crackles through the line, and I feel a pang of sympathy. "I can't just leave her there."

"I don't know…" I fish for something to keep her busy, then kick myself for not thinking of it sooner.

"Can you call Taka? Let him know what's happening? I don't want him seeing it on TV."

She curses. "Yeah, I'll call him. He's going to be scared as fuck. Shit."

"She's okay," I stress again. "She's alive, she's safe for now, and Priya's keeping me up-to-date on her condition. We know exactly where she is, and she's the top priority for rescue. As far as we know, she's the only victim trapped inside."

"She has the shittiest luck of any person I know, I swear."

"It could be better."

She lets out a slow breath, and I hear a car door open and shut. The radio comes to life, blocking out the sounds of the city. "I'll call Taka. You'll let me know if anything changes?"

"If I can get away, I'll call you."

"Thank you, Riley."

I shove my phone back into my pocket, my hands sweaty inside my gloves. As I take a spot in the human chain again, I reach out for Priya. Her presence washes over me like a balm and my shoulders relax at the contact.

How's our girl?

Pretty much the same, she Sends. There's a calmness to her voice that sounds forced, a professional veneer that has me wondering if things are worse than she's letting on. I know she was a doctor before she died and probably dealt with hysterical family members on more than one occasion. For a moment, I consider pushing her for more detail, but when she appears at the edge of the rubble pile, her fear written plainly across her face, I let it go.

I've been so wrapped up in my own fear that I haven't considered Priya's. She's known Kim longer than I by at least five years, and their connection is closer, more visceral, than anything Kim and I might have now or later. They have a bond that transcends life and death, one that Kim was able to follow to find Priya when they'd been torn apart. I can't imagine how this feels for her, and guilt lances through me that I haven't thought to ask earlier.

How are you doing?

When Priya's eyes meet mine, grief and fear wash over me. It feels like Sending, but instead of words, I'm drowned by a flood of emotion. It mixes with my own until I'm struggling to breathe through it. Hands numb and heart racing, I drop the piece of rubble I'm holding. The person next to me in line glares, then picks it up and passes it along without comment. Air stutters into my lungs as I take a deep breath, fighting for stoicism like a drowning man fights for the shore. After a moment, another piece of rubble falls into my hands, and I'm extra careful as I pass it down the line.

I've been better, Priya says after a long minute, her emotions muted somewhat. *I feel… so helpless. At least you can do something, Riley. I'm just… here.*

You're helping. She'd be alone down there if it weren't for you.

But she's still alone. That grief rolls through me again

and I fight back tears. *I can't even Heal her.*

I try to imagine what it would be like to see Kim but be unable to do anything to help. My heart twinges at the thought, and I wish there was something I could do to ease Priya's suffering. After a moment, I wrap my mind in calm, soothing thoughts. It helps center me, helps me distance myself from this disaster, and then I push those same feelings toward Priya. It's like Sending, but there's something different about it. A depth of understanding that can't be communicated with words alone. Instead, the emotions move between us, twisting and warping as she accepts them, then reflects them back at me. After a few minutes of quiet connection, our fears and worries fade while determination builds between us. She sighs, and it feels like peace.

Thank you, she Sends. It ripples through me, the words carried on a wave of feeling.

Of course. We're each doing our part, Priya, but we're in this together.

You're good people, Riley Cross.

A smile tugs at the corner of my mouth and I let it slip out as I continue passing rubble down the line.

Everyone here is working together to get Kim out of the bowels of the destroyed building, but Priya's the only other person—and she's still a person even if she is dead—who cares for Kim the way I do. And she's my friend, too, though I'm only now starting to know her outside of her relationship with Kim. Having someone else here who knows and feels the same depth of fear that I'm struggling to stay ahead of eases some of that worry, though only slightly. It's a refuge in a terrible storm, though, and I hold onto it as I continue to do my small part to get my partner—in every sense of the word—out of danger.

My mind glazes over with the monotony of moving debris. Someone hands me a piece of concrete or steel, and I hand it to someone else. The back and forth motion makes my arms and back ache, but I keep going, pushing past the pain. Eventually, even that fades, lost in the slow repetition of moving rocks. It gives my mind a place to rest, and I fade away from reality, distancing myself and getting lost in the physical ache instead.

A crash, followed by a rising wave of cries breaks me from my reverie. My head jerks up and toward the building. Dust billows from it, and firefighters and USAR members scramble from the wreckage. A wall's fallen in, and as I watch, the rubble shifts, then sinks deeper into the ground. The few remaining walls around the most damaged part of the building fall in with loud crashes and clouds of dust and smoke. People are yelling, but I can't make out their words over the ringing in my ears.

All I can think of is Kim. Kim trapped. Kim buried.

The emotion that whips through me is too cold to be fear or anger. It settles like a dead weight in the center of my chest, a sharp burning like ice that spreads out into my arms, hands, and fingers. Everything aches. My mind goes blank, uncomprehending. Terror so visceral, so physical that I have to swallow it down to breathe, overwhelms me.

Something in my mind cracks.

Golden light bursts from my body, a shock wave of power that sends dust away from me in a circular cloud. The rescue workers in the human chain stare at me, eyes wide, as power continues to pour from my body in waves. I open my mouth to yell, and light comes spilling out like water, splashing onto the ground until I'm standing in a golden, glowing pool. My eyes sting against the brightness growing around me. All the while, that cold, cold feeling moves its way through my veins, numbing me to everything but dark red fear and brilliant light.

Priya appears before me, her mouth open around the syllables of my name. I hear it as if from a distance, and when I meet her gaze, she backs away, terrified.

Cross?

A questing, familiar voice. The energy pouring from me settles, focuses. I close my eyes and fall into Second-Sight. The world is sketched out around me in a shifting, brilliant glow. The light pooling at my feet clings to me, splashing on the ground as I walk forward. People fall away from me, and I can't tell if they stumble back or if the power pushes them. Their ghostly shapes shimmer with fear.

Cross, is… you?

Her voice rises and ebbs in my mind. I try to answer, but my thoughts are too scattered, too lost in the energy filling my body to respond. Instead, I push with my emotions, sending a wave of relief, of fear, of love toward her.

I don't… happening. Why can… you? God… hurts.

Fear flows through me and spills out like light. Ice forms and settles in the power trailing behind me until it solidifies into sharp, jagged crystals that radiate with a cold glow.

Her voice grows, fades.

Power coalesces around me, and I reach out with my half-formed senses to pull it into my body. My blood crackles when I move, cold power like ice snapping on the surface of a river. It builds within me until I can't think past the frigid pain of it. With a rush that leaves me shaking, power pours out of me like a dam breaking and arrows for the collapsed building, disappearing into the earth. There's a faint residue of light left on the ground, like frost, but even that fades after another heartbeat, leaving darkness behind. My knees buckle, and I fall to the ground.

Priya's voice echoes in my head. *Riley! Can you hear me?*

Yes, I Send, though it makes my head pound. Everything is spinning. *What happened?*

You tell me! She comes closer but slows with a wince. *I can't come closer. Are you okay?*

I don't…. I rub my head. *I think so. I could've sworn I heard—*

I push to my feet and stumble toward the rubble. After I take a few unsteady steps, someone grabs me. I collapse against them, my legs giving out again, and I look up into the terrified face of Lieutenant Reddick.

"You got something you want to tell me, Detective?"

"What happened? Is Kim…"

She's okay, Riley, Priya Sends, and I sag farther. *The second collapse didn't get her. I'd know if she was…*

"Let's get you to an EMT, Detective," Reddick says as she helps me move toward one of the ambulances stationed near the cordon.

I want to protest, but everything spins, and I think I hear Kim's voice again, telling me to stay in bed, to get some rest. With a groan, I let Reddick help me stumble to an EMT. He urges me to sit on the step leading into the ambulance and covers my shaking body with a thermal blanket.

All the while, Kim's voice and the sound of falling rubble echoes in my mind like a glacier cracking.

CHAPTER NINETEEN

KIM

I'm surrounded by golden light. It's unlike anything I've ever seen, and I reach out to touch it, convinced I'm hallucinating. Instead, my fingers dip into the radiance like icy water. It clings to my skin as I pull away, and I flick it from my fingers to cast droplets like stars against the concrete. It's beautiful and terrifying. And somehow, I heard Cross's voice. Clear and strong, it echoed through my mind like an impossibility.

I wonder if they're signs of my changing powers, of whatever transformation I'm undergoing cascading out into the world around me… or symptoms of my head injury.

As I stare, uncomprehending, rocks scatter and skitter on the other side of the concrete slabs above me, then stop. The scree filling in the edges of my small space shifts and comes pouring in. I kick it away, pushing the rocks and piled dust into the small corners my body can't fit into so that my feet stay uncovered. A rumble from deep within the building makes me still, and for a long second, I don't breathe. The sound fades, stops, and I let out a gasp that tastes of fear.

My hair is stuck to my face, tacky with blood and dust. I squint, the light starting to hurt my head, but it fades slowly until I'm left in the all-consuming darkness again. Water drips from somewhere nearby, a quiet, methodical sound that fades into the background as I stare into the black around me.

Priya? What happened?

She appears next to me, glowing faintly blue-white. *There was another collapse. USAR is reassessing the situation.*

What was that light?

What light?

She answers so quickly, it has me frowning.

You didn't see it?

She shakes her head. *I don't know what you're talking about.*

There was… My head pounds. *Never mind.*

How are you feeling? she asks as she settles near me. The cold radiating from her makes me shiver, but I appreciate her gentle presence.

I take a moment to assess my situation. Surprisingly, I feel a bit better, hallucinations notwithstanding. My head still hurts, and the inside of my mouth feels like it's filled with grit and mud from all of the dust I've breathed in, but when I reach to feel the deep laceration on the back of my head, it's nearly healed. The blood there is thick and caked in my hair, but the wound has closed significantly and is no longer bleeding freely.

I think the Healing worked, I Send. *Though it packs a wallop. How in the hell did you do that every day?*

It took a lot of practice. Amusement trickles down our bond. *And a lot of control.*

Remind me to not fuck around with Healers in the future, okay?

Do you want to try again? You keep losing consciousness.

I can, but I think I fell asleep last time. I was so tired.

Looked like you passed out to me.

I sigh. *Okay, Mom.*

Priya goes quiet, and a part of me thinks I might have said that name earlier. My cheeks heat. *Sorry.*

It's okay. Let me know when you're going to start. I'll back you up, just in case.

Thanks.

After I take a deep, controlled breath, I pull the green power forward and let it fill my hands in a trickle. Easing it through my body in slow, careful pulls, I draw it toward my head and the ache there. Like cool, fresh water, the energy flows into my mind and winds itself around the heated pressure. The caustic tension eases a little before Priya orders me to back off.

Now that some of the pain in my head has lessened, everything else feels so much worse. The small pains are magnified now that the big one has softened. I can't get over how omnipresent it is. My muscles are cramping from the awkward position I'm forced to lie in. The concrete beneath me is hard and covered in small rocks and pieces of gravel that dig through my jacket and clothes, sharp biting teeth that drag against my skin no matter how carefully I move. My wet clothes cling to my skin, chafing as I try to find a more comfortable position.

It's cold down here, too. Priya's nearness makes it worse, but even if I were alone in the darkness, I'd be shivering. If that golden light had stayed, I'm sure I'd see my breath fogging the air in front of me. Its moisture clings to my face and chapped lips. Drawing my tongue across their surface, I taste blood and dirt and desperation.

I can't even take solace in the half-light of Second-Sight. The spinning, shifting colors make pain erupt like fireworks of bright, stinging misery.

At least my thoughts are clearer. I take some comfort in that, though they still come and go, fading like early-morning light, like fog, like breath exhaled into cold air.

I shiver and curl tighter around myself.

How are things going up top? I ask Priya. *If they're getting closer to pulling me out of this hellhole, that would make my day.*

Priya winces, a tangled mess of emotions dancing between us before she can suppress its echo across our bond. After a long moment—she's Sending with Cross, I assume—she responds. *The additional collapses stopped everything. Structural engineers are trying to figure out if they need to shore anything else up or if they can start removing debris again.*

You said Cooper was able to walk out of here, I Send. God, it stings... *Can't USAR get me from the same exit point?*

That's the plan right now. Cool fingers on my brow. *But*

they have to make sure it's safe to remove rubble and bring other first responders into the building. Once they can do that, they'll start digging you out, I promise.

How long, Priya?

I hate how my voice shakes. Hate the fear and vulnerability in the tone.

Priya shushes me. *Soon, I promise. They're all doing what they can to get you out of here as fast and as safely as possible.*

I curse. *I know that, but this sucks.*

Yeah. It does.

I close my eyes, though it doesn't change what I see. It's pitch black, the color darker than anything I've ever seen before. There's nothing down here. Nothing. It's all encompassing, a terrifying endless void that comes to an abrupt halt under my questing fingers as they hit the walls of my concrete tomb. I can't see my hand, can't sense where anything is around me. I'm reminded, time and time again, that even though my eyes tell me there are no boundaries to this place, they're only inches from my face.

White spots dance across the blackness. I can't tell if they're from the hit to my head or if my brain is trying to make sense of the lack of stimulation. As I watch the moving shapes, they start to twist and morph, turning from blobs to lines, then back again. Something like eyes stares back at me from the dark, and I drop into Second-Sight, fear choking my throat. As the world bursts to life around me in bright lines of color, I let out a shaky breath as I take in the wall of concrete, mundane and unmoving, in front of me.

Tell Cross… I trail off, uncertain about what I need from him at this moment. I'm desperate for contact, for something other than Priya's cold, whisper-soft touch. I want to be wrapped up in the warm comfort of his arms, my face pressed into the curve of his neck where it meets his shoulder, his scent heavy in my nose as I breathe him in. I want his hands in my hair, want to be curled into the safety of his body instead of the meager protection of my jacket. I want to be back in my bed, the early-morning light creeping through my window as we bury ourselves under blankets and each other.

Tell him I need him, I say, settling for most of the truth.

I'll let him know, Priya Sends. Worry passes between us, tinged with heartache and fear. *And I'll be right back, okay?*

Okay.

I swallow in the silence. I listen carefully and hear the remains of the building groan around me, a wounded beast settling into death. Steel and concrete slowly buckle beneath the heavy power of gravity, my soft, too easily broken body trapped within.

I'm getting maudlin and I hate it. I blame it on the darkness, on the head wound, on my exhaustion. I'm not someone to give up, to stop fighting. Biting back my fear and urge to cry, I reach for my Healing again, wanting to do something while I wait for Rescue.

But as I take the power in my hands, I hear something. A soft sound, like an exhalation from the other side of the concrete behind my back.

Priya?

There's no response, but the sound grows. It's wet, strangled.

"Hello?"

My voice is deadened in the small space, bouncing back to me, too loud and jarring in the silence. Rocks shift and skitter.

"Hurts." The voice is deep and full of gravel, too indistinct for me to tell if it's a man or a woman. Their words are garbled, almost indistinct. "So cold."

"Hey," I yell again, my heart suddenly racing. "Hey, I'm a police officer. My name is Kim Phillips. What's your name?"

"Rivera." The words are carried on a cough, followed by a wheeze that doesn't seem to end. It grates, on and on, high-pitched and dragging, as if the air is scraping its way through Rivera's lungs.

Why does that name sound so familiar? My head aches, and I push the thought away before shouting again. "Are you hurt? Can you tell me where you are?"

"Hurts," Rivera moans.

"Where are you hurt?"

Silence.

Shit.

I drop into Second-Sight and shuffle around in the small void I'm trapped in. My knee catches on a broken piece of concrete, and my pants snag, then tear, as I turn. Warm blood runs down my leg as I get to my back, then turn over so I'm facing the concrete slab my back had been against. As I strain my senses past the barrier, I can make out a broken form outlined in shifting light. It's vaguely human shaped, though I can tell that whoever it is has multiple broken bones.

"Rivera?" I shout. "Can you still hear me?"

More silence.

Priya! I Send a frantic call down our bond, and, finally, she appears by me, her hair spread out in a glowing halo around her face, her eyes flashing white.

Are you okay? What happened?

There's someone trapped in here with me, I Send, pointing toward the figure. *On the other side of the concrete. Name's Rivera, and they're hurt. Bad.*

Let me check, Priya says before floating through the concrete. *I searched the area earlier and didn't see anything, but it's a mess. I could've missed someone.*

She moves to the other side of the barrier and freezes. *Kim.*

As I watch, the figure shifts, its body lifting in a roll of broken bones and malformed muscle. Its head twists, unnaturally limp and jerking, to face Priya. It glows with a sickly red light that grows the longer I stare at it, horrified.

I can sense the rot now. The ache I've been feeling isn't only physical, it's also the electric sting of red-black, of corruption leaking into Life. It ripples beneath my skin in waves of burning pain that blends with my physical discomfort, the two sensations tangled together so closely that I couldn't separate them until now.

Staring at the fractured form before me, the difference is suddenly, terrifyingly clear.

It reaches for Priya, but either rubble or its own broken body stop it. The raised arm is bent awkwardly, sagging in the middle, the hand a mess of red-black flesh and broken bones.

Hurts, its voice whispers in my mind. *Why?*

Priya backs up, power flaring in a burst of light that makes my head pound. *You'd better shield, Kim. It's moving.*

I pull power in a rush. The energy floods my body, but my head throbs and I gag. I fight back nausea as fear overpowers the urge to vomit. Light flickers into my hands, then moves out in a wall of blue-white around me. Though I'm pouring power into it, the shield doesn't extend more than an inch from my body. When I push, trying to make it larger, gray creeps into the edges of my vision even though everything is black. I pull back, let the energy rest just outside of my skin, as the Turned ghost moves toward me.

It's not much protection, but it'll have to be enough. I don't have the strength to do more.

Slowly, it drags itself through the rubble. As it draws closer, it shines brighter, the red somehow both dark and light—a bloody, stygian color, one that shouldn't exist but somehow does. The ghost gains clarity in its shape, though that does little to help my growing fear. Hair hangs limp and dirty over its face. Its body is broken and crushed, smashed into pieces held together by memory and stubborn sinew. Motions jerky and insectile, it moves through the concrete as if it weren't there, seeping into the small space between me and the wall.

I scramble back, eyes wide, as it turns its face toward mine.

Everything about the creature is visible now: jaw broken and hanging open, tongue bloated and falling from its mouth as a purple, swollen worm. The rotten muscle moves over the ghost's lips, leaving a trail of blood behind. Its head tilts to the side, hair parting around its face, and its filmy eyes meet mine. Maggots swim behind them, shifting in the sclera in wriggling lines of off-white. Thin triangles of black cover the lower half of its eyes, bisecting the orbs like dark stains. One of its hands reaches for my face, the fingers shattered and chewed up like ground meat. Bone gleams white and sharp from the appendage, and when it touches my shield, sparks explode between us.

The creature rears back, broken limbs jerking with the motion. The dark slashes in its eyes grow until the inky darkness covers everything in a thick, impenetrable black, still shifting with bloated white bodies behind the stains.

Why? it hisses, fractured hand pulled back toward its face as if to protect itself. *Why?*

Power rolls over me in a wave of red-black. I'm drowning in it, the pressure of it against my shield as heavy as concrete and steel. I fall out of Second-Sight as I fight to keep my shield up. Power pours into it, and my head throbs. I gag, but I keep pushing, keep fighting.

Eventually, the ghost stops. It cowers, whimpering softly by the concrete slab. After a moment filled with the sounds of its wet, crushed breathing and the quiet churn of maggots moving under its skin, it fades and disappears.

What. The actual. Fuck.

Are you okay? Priya asks frantically as she settles over me, her hair still thrown about in an invisible wind.

I let my shield drop and fatigue floods my body. *Yeah,* I Send, though it's quiet and my head pounds with the strain. *But who the hell was that?*

I think, Priya says hesitantly, *that it was the body you came to investigate.*

It Turned really fucking fast.

They've been doing that lately.

Sarcasm is not appreciated, Priya. You've gotta tell Cross, and then you've got to get Taka or, hell, even Banks here as soon as possible. If there's a Turned ghost down here with me, this situation just got a hundred times more dangerous.

As soon as I stop Sending, I groan. Pain lances through me again, and I reach for my head, feeling fresh blood seeping from the cut. I'm using too much energy, pushing my body too hard, too fast.

Stars.

Sparks.

Shit.

Chapter Twenty

Priya

I don't know what to do. Kim is groaning on the ground, her hand pressed to her head again. I send Healing energy down our bond and feel an answering pulse from her. Green light grows beneath her fingers, and the pained, furrowed area between her brows eases.

God, I'm tired, she Sends.

I know. I glance around us, looking for the Turned ghost but not finding anything. *I can keep watch if you want to rest.*

I'm tired of resting. She groans. *But I think I need to. Tell Cross to get Taka here. We need backup.*

Okay. I'll keep watch.

After raising a small shield around Kim's huddled form, I reach out for Riley and feel his answering connection.

I don't want you to freak out, I Send, thinking back to the way his body filled with light after the second collapse, his eyes black in the pale expanse of his face. *But we have a problem.*

His fear lances through me. *What is it? Is Kim okay?*

You know how you two were called out here to investigate a body?

Yes, Priya. Get to the point.

It's here, and it's Turned.

Fuck. Fear, again, though this time it's tainted with anger. *How bad?*

Good news, it didn't hurt her. Bad news, I think it wants to. I'm keeping watch while Kim rests, but this thing is angry, and I don't know when it's coming back.

So, what do we do?

Get Taka, I Send. *And anyone else he can find. If any other Burners in the city can get down here, that would be great. Kim's in no shape to take care of this ghost on her own.*

There's a long pause, punctuated only by flashes of Riley's fear. Then, *Okay, I'll call Andrea. She called earlier, and I told her to fill Taka in on the situation. I'm sure they'll both want to be here now. Tell Kim we're coming, okay?*

Of course.

The Turned ghost, Rivera, is nowhere to be seen, but I can sense it like decay on the wind. Its corruption rasps against me like rusted metal, tearing at my body with minuscule teeth and claws. Shivering, I search for it in the wreckage, but only find its corpse. I trail my hands over the parts of the body that I can reach, trying to assess what I can.

I split my focus between continuing to power my shield around Kim and using it to investigate the ruined body before me. I let my power spill into the cadaver, using what little Healing I still have to try to determine the cause of death. It's hard to differentiate the pre- and postmortem injuries. The building collapse has ruined what remained of the already decaying body. Putrescence leaks from the bloated and ruptured skin. Innumerable bones are broken like matchsticks. The head is a flattened mess, crushed under the weight of a steel support beam. But deep within the body, almost lost among the metal from the building, is a tiny flash of something foreign. Not steel or copper wire, but lead.

A bullet.

I reach into the ruined remains of the body and touch my ethereal fingers to the piece of metal. It's lost somewhere in the collapsed buttresses of the corpse's rib cage. Center of mass.

It reminds me of Dominguez with four gunshot wounds to the chest.

It reminds me of his missing friend, Francisco.

Francisco Rivera.

Riley, I Send hesitantly, *I think I know who this is.*

Hold on, Priya. I'm on with Andrea.

While I wait for Riley, I try to remember what Rivera's mother had said the day before. How long it had been since she'd seen her son, and whether or not the bloated corpse we'd seen that morning would fit the timeline. Did she say two days or three? Longer?

Bloat takes a few days to set in, but it had been warm and wet in the boiler room. That would've sped up decomposition, but would it have sped it up enough to account for the length of time that Rivera was missing?

Okay, what's going on?

How long was Rivera missing? I ask, still unable to remember what his mother said.

Riley pauses. *What?*

Francisco Rivera, one of Dominguez's known associates. You and Kim tried to interview him, but his mother said she hadn't seen him for a few days. How long?

I don't… Give me a moment.

I wait again, eyes roaming the rubble for any signs of the Turned ghost. Its conspicuous absence makes me nervous, and I flinch whenever I see movement. Each time, it's rubble settling, shifting within the confines of the ruins.

Less than a week, Riley finally reports back. *Why does Rivera matter?*

Kim said the Turned ghost's name was Rivera. And based on how decomposed the body was when we arrived, it would fit with how long he's been missing.

Wait, Riley says, and I feel a burst of excitement and confusion along with his words, *you think the body here was Francisco Rivera's?*

Yes.

Shit. Another pause. *I'm going to call Martinez. Let me know if anything changes down there. Taka and Andrea are on their way.*

Left in the dark and the silence, I hover close to Kim as she rests. The only noise is the occasional groan from the ruined building. I stare into the darkness, reaching with my senses and hoping to find the Turned ghost lost in the broken steel and concrete around us. Emptiness echoes back, tinged with red-black power.

It feels like an hour passes before Riley contacts me again, though it's likely been less than that. It's hard to judge the passage of time in Death, and with nothing to signal the time of day in the darkened ruins, the distortion is worse than usual.

Taka and Andrea are here, he Sends, *and USAR is ready to move into the basement hallway that Cooper used to get out of the building. We're sending Claire down to join you, but we'll need you to keep the Turned ghost away from the rescue workers if you can.*

Understood.

A moment later, I'm joined in the darkness by Taka's partner, Claire. She looks younger than me, her pale skin and hair making her look washed out in the gray scale of Death. Her eyes are the same, solid gray as mine, though they flash with white when she approaches.

What are we dealing with here? she asks, looking around the rubble.

I give her as much information as I can, though she's as uncertain as I am when we fail to see any signs of Rivera's ghost. We're stronger together than we are separately, though, and she bolsters my shield before sitting near Kim. I hover opposite her, waiting.

You two have the worst luck, Claire says with a smile. *Taka never gets into this kind of trouble.*

I'm sure he gets into his own kind of trouble, I say.

She laughs. *That's one word for it.*

Can I ask you something?

You just did, she says, turning her head to look at me. *What do you want to know?*

After you died, I begin, discomfort rising as I broach the subject, *what was it like?*

Claire gives me a long, considering look. At first, I think that will be all the response she'll give, but then she looks away and starts speaking.

It was a long time ago, she says. *I was young when I died, and Taka was young when we Bonded. I honestly don't remember most of the details, other than pain and shock. But it was…* she trails off. *I didn't understand what had happened. It wasn't until after Taka that I learned I'd died of a stroke, completely unexpected for someone my age.*

Did you Turn?

I started to, she says. *We all do, but you know that.*

And now?

Her eyes flash black, the only answer to the question I need.

How do you fight it? I gesture to the world around us, to the power that covers every inch of it in darkness. *How do you not give in?*

I wasn't a Medium, she says gently. *I'm more powerful now than I was alive, even without giving in. And I remember those early days when I was losing myself to it. I don't ever want to *repeat that time, so I fight it. I refuse to let it win.*

I take a moment, considering her words, then plunge forward into the awkward question I haven't had the courage to ask her until now.

Why won't Taka talk to Kim about Ruth?

Her eyebrows rise. *Why does it matter?*

Have you been paying attention when Kim's come over to talk?

No more or less than I usually do. She shrugs. *It depends on the day.*

What about the red energy? You've heard her talk about that?

Claire falls silent. Then, finally, *Yes.*

Ruth is wrapped up in it. She knows something about what's happening. We need to talk to her.

You shouldn't concern yourselves with it, Claire says with finality.

What's that supposed to mean? I gesture around us at the tendrils of the red-black energy that tangle their way through the wreckage. *It's everywhere. It was always in Death, but now it's in Life, and it's getting worse. It's breaking through the barrier between the two. How can that not concern you?*

There are other people taking care of it. You both need to trust Taka.

I still. *You know what's happening.*

She turns her back to me, her short hair floating around her face with the motion.

Claire, I press. *We have to know.*

She looks back at me, and her eyes fill with white light. Her short hair floats around her face in a nimbus of tangling strands, and when she speaks, her voice is full of power.

You don't get to make demands of us. You may have been older when you died than I was, but I have been in Death longer than you by decades. I've seen things that would make you run screaming, looking for safety when there is none. Taka knows what he's doing, and until he believes you are both ready to learn more, he and I aren't telling you anything. You are both children and you need to mind your place.

I bristle at her words. Black char starts to creep over my fingers, my skin parting and crackling in bloody rivulets as it covers my hands and moves to my wrists. I clench my teeth and my hands, forcing the Turning back.

I still taste ash on my tongue.

You have no idea what our place is, I spit. *Kim is unique. You and I both know that. Taka does, too. She deserves to understand what's happening with that power and with her own.*

Claire turns away again but not before I see black explode in her right eye like a broken blood vessel, the side of her face going limp.

Don't press me on this, Priya. Her back is still turned, shoulders taut and voice icy. *When it's time, Taka will talk to Kim. Until then, stop pushing.*

I'm about to speak again when we both hear a groan and freeze. There's a wet breath near my ear, and I spin around, face-to-face with Rivera's ghost.

Priya! Claire shouts and throws a ball of energy

toward the Turned ghost. It twists out of the way, its broken body lending itself to the uncoordinated and jerking motion. As it falls away, it disappears from sight. Meanwhile, the energy flashes past me and barrels into a bent steel support beam. There's another groan, though this time it comes from the building as it shifts.

Careful! I shout. *You're going to bring this place down on top of her!*

Kim lifts her head, eyes wide and unfocused in the darkness. *Priya, what's going on?*

It's Rivera. Watch out.

We've got to stop it, Claire says to me. *It could hurt her or the rescue crews.*

So could we.

Her eyes are wide, one covered with a fractal of broken vessels that have bled black into the white of her eye. *Then what do we do?*

Bolster her shield, I Send before pouring more energy into the protective bubble around Kim. *It's newly Turned, which means it might still have some humanity left. Tell Taka what's going on while Kim and I try to figure this out, and watch our backs.*

I shift my focus to Kim. *Any chance you could convince it to leave us alone?*

I can try, she says as she rolls onto her side. *Where'd it go?*

No idea.

Unhelpful, but okay. Let me see if I've got chalk on me. Shit.

She fumbles through her pockets while Claire and I

stand guard. After a moment, she flashes a feral grin and pulls a small piece of white chalk from her pocket. It's a tiny stub, one that I can barely see past the edge of her fingers, but it's better than nothing.

I can't see for shit, she tells me. *Unless you know how to get light down here, you're going to have to walk me through scribing a circle.*

What do you want it to do?

Trap the ghost, if we can. Nothing too fancy. I don't have the strength right now to power a complicated circle. But it needs to be strong. Whatever we make, it'll be small. More a snare than anything more substantial.

Okay. I think rapidly, mind spinning. *I have an idea.*

I float close to the ground, find a relatively dry patch, and start pouring power into the tip of my pointer finger. The energy builds until my skin glows as if lit from within. When I drag my finger over the ground, it leaves a trail of light behind. After a few moments, I have a basic binding circle scribed. Kim smiles at me from the darkness, her eyes distant as she looks at the marks on the ground.

Something growls from deep within the building, and we meet each other's eyes, fear trailing skeletal fingers down my spine.

That'll work for now.

She starts tracing the marks, adjusting them slightly as she goes. After another minute, she has the circle scribed in chalk. She lets the final bit of the chalk drop from her fingers, so small it's immediately lost in the gravel spread across the broken concrete beneath her.

I turn to Claire. *Anything you want to add?*

No. She shakes her head. *Get the circle powered, and let's see if we can't catch this thing.*

What's Taka doing?

He's talking to Detective Cross. Her eyes go vague and distant, brow furrowed. *Taka says he doesn't look good.*

Kim tenses. *What happened?*

No idea, Claire says honestly. *But he's in the back of an ambulance.*

Priya, Kim Sends, shocked, *what happened?*

It's hard to explain, I hedge, *but he'll be fine, I promise. We need to focus on the Turned ghost right now. That's the bigger danger.*

Kim frowns but nods reluctantly. *I can't get my knife out of my boot to make the cut, and I'm weak, so this is going to be a pretty shaky binding. It won't hold for long. With the confined space*—she nods to the small space she's trapped in—*we're going to have to act fast once it's trapped. Be on your guard.*

Understood.

She reaches for her knee. Blood streaks her leg, and there's a long cut that's clotted at the joint. Fingers fumbling in the dark, she digs into the cut, forcing the wound open again. Red beads, and she smears her fingers through it before pressing them to the chalk.

The binding shimmers to life, flickering like a candle flame in the wind. After a moment, the three of us watching it with anxious eyes, the glow steadies. Kim lets out a heavy sigh.

Now, we just have to find it, Claire says.

I spin in a slow circle, eyes wide as I search for Rivera's ghost, but there's nothing, only darkness threaded through with red-black light.

You see it, Claire? I ask, still scanning the area.

Nothing, she Sends back, *but I can feel it.*

I can, too. Its corruption tears at the edge of my senses, and though I turn in that direction and reach for the spirit, there's nothing there.

Do you think it's disguising itself somehow? Kim asks. *I mean, I thought it was still alive when it first reached out.*

Maybe, I Send back. *It could blend into the wreckage. The body was barely recognizable when I found it. The ghost may be the same.*

We fall silent. I stretch out with my senses, questing for Rivera's presence when, suddenly, it appears.

There, I Send before arrowing toward the creature.

It lifts itself up, lurching its broken body to face me. Appearing from the tangled lines of Second-Sight in a twisted mass, its form becomes clearer as it takes a shambling step toward me. Black, writhing eyes meet mine, and it grins through its broken teeth.

Why? it asks, and the sound of its voice grates like gravel in my mind.

Try to herd it toward the circle, Claire says, flying to the other side of the creature. *We need to contain it before it disappears again.*

It lunges for me before she's fully in position, and I have to dodge away from the creature's broken, grasping fingers. It falls forward, unable to catch itself on its shattered arms, and then rolls. Its bloated body warps as it comes into contact with the ground, internal organs and fractured bones sloshing within its putrefying skin like a bag full of water. I expect it to burst open, but, instead, the creature wrenches itself to its feet before lunging again.

Drive it toward the circle, I shout to Claire as I dodge.

The creature stays somewhat upright, its waist twisted and its arms hanging at odd angles by its sides. *Hurts,* it hisses, bloated tongue writhing in its mouth.

A blast of energy from Claire sends the creature rocking forward, and it turns its head toward her, bones cracking with the motion. It screams, and red-black power courses out of its mouth in a shock wave that sends her flying back with a cut-off scream.

Priya! Kim shouts, her body curled as far away from the circle as she can get it. *Hurry!*

I gather power in my hands, my hair floating around my head in a tousled mass, then throw it at the creature. It whips around, eyes black, and stumbles toward me with supernatural speed. Caught off guard, I lurch backward, avoiding its outstretched arm. As it opens its mouth to scream again, I zip past the circle in front of Kim. The ghost, too caught up in its desire to catch its attacker, reaches toward me, broken jaw hanging open as it pants after me, and its hand crosses the thin, bright barrier of the binding.

The creature keeps lunging for me, but its arm stays trapped within the light. As it's drawn up short, it looks back at its hand, then jerks at it angrily. The binding flares but holds. The creature thrashes and writhes, but the binding refuses to let go of its hand. Even with its broken bones and skin, the appendage stays connected to the rest of Rivera's body.

Slowly, the wrenching stops. Broken mouth open, breath panting from collapsed lungs, it turns its bloated, maggot-infested face toward Kim. It leans forward, and black blood drips from its lips to splash onto the shield tight around Kim's body. It dribbles down, hissing and casting off steam until it drops to the floor, leaving a faint, dark trail across the glowing blue-white light.

Hello, it whispers, *Burner.*

CHAPTER TWENTY-ONE

RILEY

Martinez is less than thrilled when I talk to him. He curses into his phone quietly as I explain that the body is Francisco Rivera's.

"That's bad news, Riley," he says. "Really fucking bad news. That means whoever is leading this shit is cleaning house. He's on the run, and if we don't catch him soon, he's going to get away with all of this."

"I don't know what you want me to do," I say, quickly growing annoyed as I shiver in the back of the ambulance. "We need Kim."

"How close are they to getting her?" he asks.

I glance at the building. A USAR team, their navy blue jumpsuits turned gray by dust, is gathered by the entryway that Officer Cooper stumbled from earlier. After they smack each other on the top of their bright orange hard hats, they disappear into the bowels of the building.

"Shit, they're going in right now," I say. "I've gotta stop them."

"What? I thought you wanted them to get Phillips

out of there."

"There's a Turned ghost down there with her," I say as I clamber to shaky feet. "I didn't think they were going in so soon."

"You go handle that. But once Phillips is out and cleared, get a sketch artist or something down there so we can get an ID on the shooter. I'd be shocked if she isn't put on medical leave after this, and we need to catch this guy before it's too late."

Though I hate the idea of putting more pressure on Kim after everything else, I agree. "Line up the resource. I'll make sure they get to Kim."

"Stay safe, Riley, and call me if anything changes."

"Will do," I say as he hangs up.

I slip my phone back into my jacket pocket, fingers trembling. I catch sight of Reddick and wave her down. She starts heading my way, but not fast enough for my liking, so I stumble over to her, holding the thermal blanket tight.

"Detective Cross," she says, brow furrowed. "You should be resting. Whatever happened earlier, it apparently took a lot out of you, and I don't need another casualty on my hands."

"Ma'am," I say, "with all respect, you need to pull that team back. There's a Turned ghost in the building."

She's unshaken by the news. "Is it an immediate danger?"

"I'm not sure, but I don—"

"Is it currently in contact with your partner?"

"No, it's hiding somewhere in the structure."

She nods. "Then we're going to move forward with this rescue operation, Detective. The structure has been shored, we know where our victim is, and we know that she needs medical attention. Our teams have been trained to handle ghosts, and this isn't the first scene where we've encountered them. As long as they have ample warning, they'll be fine. Now, please." She takes my elbow and starts leading me back to the ambulance. "You're more use to me rested. Get some medical treatment, and when we have your partner out, I'll come find you."

I nod, clearly outclassed, and let her settle me on the back step of the ambulance bay. When she goes to help me climb inside, I wave her away.

"Here's fine," I say. "Thank you, Lieutenant."

She unclips a heavy-duty radio from her belt and offers it to me. "Take this. If anything changes down there, you let me know. The rescue team is using channel three."

"Of course." I set the radio down on the floor of the ambulance, the weight of the device making my arm tremble. Reddick watches the movement, then waves over an EMT.

"Get him checked out, will you?"

The young man looks chagrined. "I've been trying, but he won't let me."

"Detective," she says, sounding like my mother, "take care of yourself, or I'm ordering you to leave the scene. Do you understand me?"

I nod and wait for the EMT to check my vitals. Reddick gives the scene an approving gaze, then heads back toward the command center with a curt goodbye.

The EMT checks my blood pressure, heart rate, and oxygen levels. Listening to my chest with a stethoscope, he frowns the whole time and announces that my vitals are fine, though it doesn't make any sense to him. He offers me a protein bar, which I turn down, and a small container of orange juice, which I drink in a few quick sips.

Even with the thermal blanket wrapped around my shoulders, I'm freezing. The April air, heavy with moisture and cold, bites through the reflective plastic, my body heat sucked away with every wet gust. I'm exhausted yet don't know why it would all catch up to me now. I've been pushing myself all day, sure, but I did have a good night's sleep. Though my muscles ache, it's a familiar pain, almost comfortable. My mind, however, is lost in a haze. When I try to focus, my vision blurs or goes double. Although the EMT suggests starting IV fluids, I push him off. If I have a needle in my arm, it's going to slow me down from getting to Kim when they finally reach her. And even though I'm dead on my feet, there's no way I'm not going to her as soon as she's safe.

Someone calls my name, and I jerk my head up to scan the crowd. After a moment, I make out a familiar form hurrying in my direction. Taka is nearly running, his slim shoulders covered in a heavy jacket and his expression as violent as a Midwestern thunderstorm.

"What has happened?" he snaps once he makes eye contact with me.

"Gas explos—" I start, but he cuts me off.

"Andi told me on the way what happened to Kim. I meant what has happened to *you*. I could sense the power radiating from you as soon as we arrived."

Confused, I reach for my power and find that Taka is right. It's spilling from me in great, invisible waves. When I drop into Second-Sight, bright, golden light covers the ground all around me like a lake of power. I try to pull it back, but it bucks my control and continues slowly spreading into an ever-widening circle.

"I'm not doing it. I don't…" I swallow. "I can't pull it back."

Sharp footsteps hurry toward us, and Andrea appears behind Taka. Her normally neat hair has fallen from its ponytail and cascades in tight ringlets around her face. She brushes it back as she approaches, but the black corkscrews bounce back, covering her reddened cheeks.

"What the hell is going on, Detective?" she asks.

"He is out of control," Taka snaps. "And it is draining him."

I want to protest, but my vision blurs again. "How do I stop it?"

"You do not," he says. "Andi, we will have to do something."

"Taka," she says, stunned. "That seems unnecessary. Detective Cross can do this on his own if we guide him."

"I am doubtful of that, especially under these circumstances. Unless he can control his power, he will be a danger to himself and others."

"But you can't take the choice from him," she says, anger quickly coloring her tone. "He's not a child."

"As far as his power is concerned, he is an infant. He cannot care for himself, so we must."

I hold up my hand, cutting off Andrea's angry reply. "Stop. None of this is important. Kim is trapped down there with a Turned ghost, and that needs to be our primary focus."

"Claire will inform me if there is an issue," Taka says dismissively. "Until we can reach Kim, you and your lack of control are my primary concerns."

"You can't be serious," Andrea says.

Taka quells her with a look.

Sighing, I drift into Second-Sight. The golden power surrounding me has grown while they've fought, and it flows out of me as I watch, dropping with splashes of light into the pool at my feet. I follow the bright trail of energy up my legs and torso to my chest, where it seeps from my scar. It blazes, visible though it's covered by my clothes. I lift a trembling hand to the raised mark on my skin, feeling its edges underneath my dress shirt. When my fingers meet the power gathered there, it flashes so bright I have to close my eyes. A luminous halo remains behind my eyelids, a circle quartered by a cross with one arm longer than the others.

A symbol for Burners. A symbol for Kim. It's tied me to her more tightly than anything else, a physical reminder her touch, her blood, left carved into my skin. She saved my life and changed it with one action, and as I watch the gathered power beneath me shimmer to the tempo of my pulse, I can't help but think that she is, in some way, the cause of this, too.

"Once Kim is safe," I say, surprised at how quiet my voice is, "I think it will stop."

"And why do you think this?" Taka asks. "She is not responsible for your power."

"Actually," I say, my mouth tilting up into a small smile, "I think she is."

"Then you would be wrong." Taka's voice cuts through me, and the smile on my face vanishes. "She is not your Mentor, and as Andrea says, you are not a child. Unless you can stop this now, you are putting everyone around you at risk. Do you seriously think an *onryou* would not take advantage of this power? That it would not use this energy to hurt those around it?"

I honestly don't know. Donna hasn't taught me much about Turned ghosts, and my limited experience with them has only taught me to run the other way when one shows up. Trusting Taka's decades of experience, I shake my head, my hand still pressed to my scar. Power leaks through my fingers, spilling over my skin to drip into the pool at my feet.

"You're right," I force out. "But I can stop it. Just… give me a minute."

I shut my eyes. Darkness swallows me. Cut off from

sight, I can feel the power oozing from me. It tickles as it travels over my fingers, cold and clinging. When I clench the fabric of my shirt in my fist, it sticks together, as if the fabric is wet in the physical as well as the supernatural world. Past the thin, starched cotton, I sense an ache, almost like a wound, in my chest. Reaching for it in the same way I Send or use Second-Sight, I find something. It's almost like a gap or a hole in the very center of my scar. Isolated to the intersection of the arms of the cross, there's an emptiness within my skin, a lack that I wouldn't have sensed if Taka hadn't made me look for it.

Frowning, I press a finger against it, damming the flow for a brief moment before it wells beneath my skin, then forces its way past the blockage to ease its way down my chest. I concentrate, gathering the energy coating my finger and focusing on it. It sings to something within me, and after a moment, I imagine it solidifying, freezing in place. Ice cracks through me, but when I pull my finger away from my skin, the power remains, caught within a frozen cage.

I shift and feel whatever barrier I erected strain with the motion. It's thin and brittle but firmly closed over the wound. I can tell it's only a stopgap, though. Hopefully, Kim will be out of danger before it fails.

"There," Taka says, sounding both annoyed and pleased. "Now that *that* is done, we must focus on the Turned ghost with Kim."

My energy quickly returning, I agree before sliding out of the metallic blanket. "Kim and I are investigating a homicide, and the ghost is a known associate of our victim. His body was in the building before it collapsed. It's why she was here in the first place."

"While this is fascinating information, it is not important for what we need to do. Tell me, what are its powers? How has it manifested?" Taka asks.

Andrea nods. "If we know how it's attacking, we can target our defenses and approach to containing and Burning it."

"Priya hasn't said." I look between the two of them. "What about your partner?" I ask Taka.

His eyes go distant and he frowns. "Claire is not responding." He turns his attention to Andrea. "Assume the worst and start preparing protections for the crowd."

"Understood," Andrea says. "I'll start scribing and find you when it's ready."

"And you"—Taka gives me a quick, dismissive look—"you will stay out of the way."

"The hell I will." I get to my feet, any lingering fatigue washed away by a wave of annoyance. "I may not know everything about your world, but I'm here to help. Tell me what to do and I'll do it."

His expression softens, suddenly tired and sad in a way that I don't understand. Taka wears his age well, but, for a flash, the wrinkles cutting their way across his face grow and deepen, the gravity of time weighing heavy on him. Yet his shoulders straighten, strength and determination filling his frame, and the brief moment of vulnerability is gone.

"Assist Andi," he says. "She is incredibly talented but will need blood with power to start and hold the circle. That will be your role."

I open my mouth to protest, but he holds up a hand, stopping the words before they can escape.

"You are an Apprentice. In this, you will do as you are told. Until you learn to listen, learn to take direction from those who know more than you, you will be a risk that I cannot afford. Do you understand me?"

I'm cold again, though there's no wind gusting through the parking lot. Muscles stiff with tension, I nod, then brush past Taka toward Andrea.

I can sense his eyes on my back the entire way.

CHAPTER TWENTY-TWO

KIM

The Turned ghost's breath is rancid, and as it licks its bloated tongue across its lips, a maggot crawls from the soft interior of its mouth and falls onto my shield. Though small, the weight adds strain to the thin layer of protective energy, and I swipe a trembling hand across my cheek, sending the spectral grub flying.

Rivera's ghost lunges for me again, broken jaw grating as it snaps its teeth toward my hand. I press my back into the concrete, teeth gritted to hold back a scream, and my pulse races as the creature laughs.

Why? it asks again. *Why are you here, Burner?*

Trust me, I say, voice shaking, *if I had any choice in the matter, I wouldn't be.*

Of course, it spits. *No one would be here. It hurts.*

It jerks against the binding again, and pain lances through my body as I try to hold the creature within. Even though the creature's hand is the only thing caught in the small circle, it's taking all of my focus to keep it locked within the light. Sweat breaks out on my forehead as the creature shakes and writhes, its broken body turning in unnatural forms that make me want to gag as much as the growing pain in my head does.

Priya, I Send with more force than necessary, *what the fuck am I supposed to do here?*

Rationalize with it, she says. *Talk it down. It's newly Turned. You might be able to Turn it back.*

Christ. Easier fucking said than done.

Rivera, I try, and the creature snarls at me, its blood-tainted teeth snapping in front of my face. *Francisco. I'm here to help.*

Burner. It draws the word out. *You don't help. You destroy.*

Fuck. I hate Turned ghosts. *I'm not trying to destroy anything, Francisco. I want to find who killed you, bring you justice.*

The creature tips its head back and howls. Red-black waves of power lash at me with each harsh, crackling peal, and I cower, arms wrapped around my head as I fight to hold the ghost at bay and keep my shield up.

Light flashes beyond the barrier of my arms, and as I peer through them, Priya flares her power, hair lashing around her head in a dark storm. The creature stumbles back, its hand holding it in place when it turns to run.

You can't bring me justice! it screams. *The only justice is the kind I take for myself.*

It tears at its hand, skin and sinew splitting beneath its scrabbling fingers. The delicate bones of its wrist, somehow undamaged by the collapse and the Turning, wink out from between the ragged edges of its skin like pink-tinged stars. Something cracks and the joint stretches.

Shit. Priya! Claire!

I reach for both of them, then gather power between my hands. The binding—crude and rushed and wildly underpowered—snaps at my fingers as it forms, and as another strand of the creature's skin tears, I wrap the binding around its wrist like a bandage of light.

The scream that erupts from its throat bursts something in my ear. A sharp pain ricochets through me, and all I can hear is a loud, endless ringing. Beneath my fingers, the binding smokes and steams, burning its way into the creature's flesh. My hand feels like it's on fire. Blisters form on my skin, then burst. I grit my teeth, holding tight through the pain while the creature shakes like a fish on a line, trying to tear itself away from my grip.

I need more power! I scream.

Priya and Claire appear on the other side of the ghost, their eyes white and glowing. They extend their arms, their fingertips brushing, as they turn their eyes to me.

Take it, they say together, their voices melded in a strange harmony.

Then power jumps from their hands, across the space, and into the binding. It glows like a sun beneath my hand. Bones cast shadows in the bloody-red outline of my fingers, and Rivera roars.

From beneath the edges of the binding, his skin

starts to knit together. Popping like corn, his bones snap and jump. Distorted and mottled skin smooths out, becoming even and supple. The binding follows behind, wrapping Rivera's slowly healing form in bright, white light. The intensity grows until I can't bear to look at him. I shut my eyes and still see his figure through the thin skin of my eyelids.

Thought it makes my head ache, I push forward, pouring my remaining energy into the binding.

Almost there, Priya Sends, her voice tight. *You can do it, Kim.*

The world starts to dim, but I keep pushing. Warm blood trickles from my nose and over my mouth, and I open it wide, breathing in rock-scented air as I fight to complete the binding. I can feel it closing, nearly complete, and elation soars through me.

No!

Rivera's voice rips through my mind, and then his wrist rips from my hand.

"Shit!" I shout, grasping at empty air.

My blistered hand scrabbles against concrete, and the only thing left of Rivera's ghost is its outline behind my eyes. I try to blink it away, desperately searching the space around me in normal and Second-Sight, but there's nothing of the man remaining.

Priya, I Send frantically. *You have anything?*

No, he's gone. Her voice shakes. *What the hell kind of ghost are we dealing with?*

I have no idea. Claire, see if Taka has seen this before, and keep your eyes open for him.

Heart racing, I focus on Healing the damage to my hand and ear. I pull power again, then slowly ease spring-green into the damaged skin of my palm. It stings as it heals, but the pain diminishes until it fades to nothing. I let the power go, then drop into Second-Sight again, searching.

How far is the rescue team? I ask Priya before lying back down on the ground, panting. I don't need to worry about ruining the binding now, and without any more chalk, there's no way to try again. *I need to know whether I can do anything to help them if Rivera attacks.*

Priya goes silent, but our bond is quickly flooded with a rush of relief. *They're not far. They've breached the doorway into the boiler room and they're heading your way.*

Thank God.

You should hear them soon, Priya says, though she sounds worried. *You'll need to make sure you don't confuse them with Rivera if he comes back.*

Crap. I hadn't thought of that. My ears are still ringing, and when I reach my hand up to touch the one where the pain was the worst, my fingers come away sticky with blood.

I think it burst my eardrum, I Send. With a flash of green, I focus more power into my ear and wait for the ringing to subside. *You know, when I'm not dealing with a major injury, this Healing stuff is pretty convenient.*

Don't underestimate that power, Kim, Priya cautions. *It's dangerous.*

I know. I pause. *How's Cross?*

He's doing better, she says. *He's with Andrea right now. She's scribing protections around the scene.*

What happened?

I don't know. He just… exploded with power. She bites her lip, then pushes her hair from her face. *The only thing I've seen like it was when we fought Baker.*

Baker's gone, I snap. *He's been gone. What's happening with Cross doesn't have anything to do with him.*

Are you sure about that? she asks gently. *We've never gotten to the bottom of how Baker was able to possess Riley in the first place, or why our previously Mundane friend is suddenly Sighted and on his way to becoming a full Medium. You can't keep ignoring the problem, Kim. It's not going to go away.*

We have bigger problems to deal with, I say, nodding toward the ruins around me. *Not to mention the missing psychotic ghost.*

I'm not psychotic, a gravelly voice says from behind my ear.

I curse, then roll onto my other side, my back against the opposite piece of concrete.

Rivera's ghost, looking much better than the last time I saw it, is sitting quietly against the pile of scree, his fingers locked around his wrist as he stares at the band of white still wrapped around it. His broken hands and arms are whole again, no longer limp and twisted, but strong and straight. His torso is covered by a white T-shirt, and though blood seeps from a small hole in the center of it, the previously ruptured flesh appears undamaged.

Be on guard, I Send in a tight pulse to Priya. *There's no telling what he's going to do.*

I'll let Claire and Taka know. I've got your back.

I turn my attention back to Rivera, who looks at me with his stained eyes from behind the heavy fringe of his hair. *Are you going to try to kill me?*

He laughs, though it's mirthless. *I don't want to kill you. You're safe, Burner.* His eyes flicker black. *For now.*

May I? I ask, reaching a hand out for the binding around his wrist. Slowly, he offers his arm to me, and when my fingers touch the light encasing him, I find it solid and strong. I let out a slow breath, then pull my hand back. *Thank you. Will you let me help you?*

How, exactly, are you going to do that? he asks. *I'm already dead.*

Someone killed you.

Yeah, no shit, he says. *What do you plan to do about it?*

Track them down, arrest them, put them in jail.

He laughs. A soft wave of red-black power flows from his mouth with the sound. It rushes over me as a stinging pain, and I shudder, unable to twist away from it.

He's a cop, Rivera says. *You won't be able to bring him down. He's got friends who'll stop you.*

I've got friends, too, I say. *And I'm also a homicide detective. Catching killers is my job no matter who they are.*

Even other cops?

Even then. My voice is firm. *If you murder someone in my city, I'm coming for you.*

He raises his eyebrows, not looking entirely convinced. But on the edges of his expression, there's a hint of respect.

Okay, Burner, he says. *How are you going to bring me justice?*

CHAPTER TWENTY-THREE

RILEY

A ndrea takes in the gathered onlookers and the first responders, then bites her lip.

"Ideally, I'd block off this entire area"—she gestures toward the plot of land where the office building is located—"but there are too many people around to do that safely. The circle will need to be tighter, but that'll make it more efficient. And if you're powering it," she adds with a rueful smile, "you're going to appreciate that a lot."

"Just tell me what you need," I say.

"A stiff drink?" When I don't laugh, she rolls her eyes. "Get these people out of the way, Detective. This is going to take some time."

It takes some careful phrasing and a heavy dose of charm to get Lieutenant Reddick to agree to Andrea's request, but between the two of us and a handful of CFD members who Reddick ropes into the exercise, we're able to clear an area of open space around the building. Because the scribing requires stone or a hard surface to work, it's not exactly a perfectly circular shape, but Andrea says it'll work for what she needs to do. After grabbing a box of chalk from her car, she gets to work.

Watching her scribe is like watching an artist. I don't know any of the symbols that she uses—unsurprising since I haven't started that part of my Medium training—but she draws them with steady, practiced fingers. They flow out of the chalk between her fingers, dust staining the tips as she scribes. Her motions almost meditative, she moves like water, like wind. There is power in her knowledge. She becomes something both natural and supernatural, her competency obvious with each curving line and sharp slash she makes against the ground.

The marks grow in complexity as we move around the perimeter, each character looping back into the one before it until the whole thing looks like a series of intersecting lines, a riotous, beautiful tangle of stark white against the black tarmac and gray sidewalk. As we near the end of the circle, she slows, then stops.

"Detective," she asks carefully, "do you know what your Affinity is yet?"

I frown. "No, not yet."

"Great." She pushes the hair away from her face, tucking it behind her ear with chalk-stained fingers and leaving a slash of white across her cheekbone. "Do you know what it isn't?"

"I'm not a Burner, and Kim and I are pretty sure I'm not a Reader or a Healer, either."

"That helps," she says and scribes a few more

symbols on the ground. "Knocks out almost half of the Affinities."

"Why do you need to know?"

"It helps make the protection more specific," she says, "which means it'll be less draining for you. It's a large circle, and if we need to use it, it's going to take a good chunk of power to keep it running. By tying it to a specific Affinity, I can channel the energy in such a way that it works in parallel with the Medium's specific power. It makes it easier for them to control it that way."

"Why not target Taka, then?" I ask. "He's a Burner. No guesswork there."

"We're going to need him to focus on the Turned ghost. He won't be able to do that and hold the circle at the same time."

"So, I'm a glorified battery?"

She shrugs. "Your words, not mine."

"How much power are we talking about here?" I ask as I take in the large swath of white marks stretching out around the perimeter of the collapsed building. When I think of how smaller circles have left Kim drained, a knot forms in the pit of my stomach.

"Do you want the technical answer, or do you want the quick and dirty one?"

"Let's stick to quick and dirty for now."

"Think of it like plugging a television in. If the TV is off, it'll still draw a tiny amount of energy from the socket. But start using it, and it draws more. The heavier the usage, the more power it needs."

"And this circle works the same way?"

"If we're talking about powering it, yes. It'll take power to start it, but not a lot. If the ghost starts testing the boundaries of it, though…"

I swallow. "It can't… drain me or anything, can it?"

"A poorly scribed circle could." She shoots me a smug look. "But this isn't a poorly scribed circle."

"I'll have to take your word for it."

"I'm not an idiot, Detective. You're new to this. You don't know your limits yet." She gestures toward the series of marks she just made. "I put in a fail-safe of sorts. The circle will be able to tell when it's drawing too much power from you, and if it does, it'll break. You'll have a hell of a headache and probably need a few days of rest, but it won't kill you."

"Okay." I start digging in my jacket pocket for my keys and the Swiss Army knife I have clipped to them. "Where do I bleed on the thing?"

"Don't get ahead of yourself," she says, gesturing for me to stop what I'm doing. "First off, we won't power it until we absolutely have to. Turned ghosts are unpredictable. We need to save our energy until it's here and attacking. Second, whatever knife you're about to pull out isn't going to be the best tool for the job. Mediums use silver for a reason. Taka's got a knife that we'll use to make any cuts we need."

"I can't say I mind putting that part of things off."

I run a hand through my hair, then offer it to her to

help her stand. She takes it firmly, leaving chalk on my palm when she pulls her hand back. Idly, I wipe it on my pants, then follow her as she walks back to Taka whose eyes are closed while CFD and USAR personnel move around him.

As we approach, he opens his eyes. "You are finished?"

"All set," Andrea says. "What's happening with Kim?"

"The ghost attacked, but she has partially bound it. They are talking now."

"Is she okay?" I ask, heart racing and the thin sheet of ice holding back my power groaning.

"She is no worse off than she was before. If anything, she is in a better position."

"Because the ghost is bound," I press.

He nods. "Because it is bound, and the rescue crews are nearly to her, according to Claire. They will have her out of the ruins soon."

"Thank God," I say with a sigh. "Let me update the team on her position. Since she's awake, she can help guide them to her."

The radio Reddick gave me is heavy on my belt, and I unclip it before transmitting on the channel the rescue teams are using.

"This is Detective Riley Cross," I say.

After a moment, the radio crackles to life. "Detective Cross, this is Rescue. Go ahead."

"I have confirmation that you're approaching

Detective Phillips's location."

"Copy, Detective. Can you give us any specifics?"

"She's conscious and can respond if you call for her."

"Copy that. We'll try to make contact and radio if we do. Over."

"One other thing, Rescue," I say, breaking protocol to keep them on comms.

"Copy, Detective."

"The Turned ghost has been partially bound. You should have some warning if it's going to attack."

"Copy that, Detective. Thank you for the information. Rescue, over and out."

I switch my radio back to the general channel and clip it to my belt before turning to Andrea. "Seems like we won't need the circle after all."

"No," Taka says firmly. "Turned ghosts cannot be trusted. They are unpredictable. A partial binding means that there will be more warning when it attacks, not that it will not attack at all."

Andrea bites her lip. "She's bought us time, but she or Taka will need to Burn the bastard if we want to guarantee no one will get hurt."

"I will," Taka says, giving Andrea a quelling glance. "She is weak and does not need the additional strain it will put on her."

"So, what do we do now?" I ask.

"We prepare," Taka says, "and we wait."

I want to sigh. Waiting is all I've been doing today.

"What can I do to help?"

Taka gives me a long, considering look and frowns. His eyes go distant, and after a minute, his sharp gaze finds me again.

"Kim is in contact with Claire, as is Priya. However, Sending to multiple people can get taxing. Stay close enough that Priya can contact you, and relay information between her and Claire while she and I get ready for the *onryou*. Andrea, you come with me. I will need your expertise." He turns and starts heading toward the chalk circle surrounding us.

"It's nearly over," Andrea says, clapping me on the shoulder as she brushes past me. "Just a bit longer, and we'll have her out of there."

I nod and turn back to the building.

Priya, I Send, searching for her presence within the rubble. *Rescue crews are on their way. They may start calling for Kim, so make sure she's paying attention.*

Of course, she replies, though her voice sounds off again. *Why wouldn't—*

She's paying attention, Riley.

I know, I Send, confused. *You just told me that.*

No, I didn't. Are you Sending to Claire?

Maybe? I reach out again, searching for the other voice. *Claire?*

There's a long pause, then a pulse of alarmed confusion. *Cross?*

Kim? I freeze.

What ar… doing? she asks.

I grasp for an answer. *Sending?*

I'm not... ghost. You shouldn... ble to Sen... me.

I'm not doing it well, I reply. *You keep dropping out.*

I guess we kn... finity is n... Couldn't b... Shit.

Riley, Priya says, interrupting the broken Sending between Kim and me. *Are you Sending with Kim?*

Seems like it, I reply uncertainly. *I'm only getting every other word from her, though.*

Priya sighs. *We'll worry about that later. We can hear the rescue crew, and Rivera's ghost is still here. Kim needs to stay focused, but I'll let you know if anything changes.*

Yeah, I say, feeling chastised. *I'll be here. Stay safe.*

Of course.

I nearly turn away from the ruins, then take a hesitant step forward. *Kim?* I Send, putting as much focus and energy into her name as I can.

I'm here. Her voice comes through the connection loud and clear.

I close my eyes as emotion sweeps over me. Elation, relief, and then an overwhelming sense of uselessness. I'm so fucking *close* to her but still as unable to do anything about it as I have been all day.

I'll see you soon, I Send, fighting for composure.

She doesn't Send back any words, only a sense of certainty, of steely determination that's all Kim. And underpinning it all, a warmth like sheets heated by skin, like her hand pressed into mine.

I embrace that feeling until it cuts out like a radio turned off, and all I can do is wait.

CHAPTER TWENTY-FOUR

KIM

T he connection to Cross cuts out, and I reach for it desperately yet stop myself, feeling like a child. Rivera, his eyes still covered with half-moons of black, watches me idly, his fingers rubbing over the bright cuff around his wrist.

Sorry, I Send, embarrassed at my weakness and fighting to regain focus. *You were saying.*

We've been running drugs through here, he continues. *It's been going on for months.*

But…?

But we never got any attention from the cops. He frowns. *I always thought that was odd, that the police never did anything about it. We were careful when we started, but not for long.*

That's when you figured out that there were officers involved in the racket.

He shakes his head. *Juan figured it out, not me. He didn't do great in school, but he was smart. Noticed things*

When did you meet the officers involved?

We never did, he says. *Just heard a name. John.*

I nod. *I've heard that name before.*

It's pretty common, Kim, Priya says quietly.

I'm hoping Martinez has one on his list. I cough, then spit. Dust clings to my lips, and I grimace at the taste of it before directing my thoughts back to Rivera.

What happened when you were killed?

His eyes flash black, and I watch as his clenched fist starts to deform, the bones cracking as the skin splits open. I blink, and his flesh rights itself, turning smooth and unbroken as his hand relaxes.

I got called here by the bosses. They didn't say why they wanted to see me, but Juan had a bad money drop a few months ago, and they made it sound like it was something like that.

I nod and gesture for him to continue. He looks at his hands, the fingers tangled together in a knot of uncertainty.

I know it's hard to talk about. I look at the bright red stain in the center of his chest. *Take your time.*

I'm just so fucking mad. His eyes flash black again. *It was some old white asshole. Figured he was security or a janitor or something. Barely even noticed him until it was too late.*

How'd you end up down here? I ask.

We always did drops down here. He looks around. *There were a bunch of storage rooms on this floor and a door that led to the old loading docks out back. Made it easy to get in and out without anyone noticing. Once I was down here, though, I knew something was wrong.* Rubbing his chest, he shakes his head. *And then it was too late.*

Francisco, I say cautiously. *One of the things that Burners do is take the final memories of ghosts who have failed to pass on. They have to be given willingly, but if you can show me what you saw before you died, I can find your killer.*

He bares his teeth at me. *And do what? Arrest him? Put him in jail?* He laughs, the sound coarse and broken. *There's no justice there. He knows how the system works, has contacts inside. He'll just go from one life to another.* A maggot crawls from the side of his mouth, then vanishes under the waterfall of his hair. *There's no justice other than what I can give him.*

It isn't the first time we've come back to this point, and Rivera isn't budging on it.

You're going to have to convince him to let go, or you're going to have to Burn him, Priya says quietly. *There's no way around it.*

I don't have any chalk with me, I Send angrily. *There's no Burning anyone right now.*

You've done it with your blood before. You can try again.

I grimace. *I really don't want to do that.*

If that rescue crew doesn't get to you soon, you may not have a choice.

How far are they again? I ask.

Not far.

I turn back to Rivera. *What does your justice look like?* I ask. *How is it any different from mine?*

Blood trickles from his mouth as he smiles. *It looks like death.*

And how is that justice? He escapes to the afterlife? Let him rot in a jail cell.

I already told you— Rivera sits up, his bones snapping before he suddenly disappears. A moment later, I hear a muffled shout that sounds like my name.

Tell me if he's coming, I Send to Priya before I move, shuffling my body until I'm facing the concrete that was against my back.

"Hello?" I yell. "Is someone there?"

"Detective Phillips?" It's louder this time though still muffled.

"Holy shit," I murmur before I press my face as close to the concrete as I can without my mouth touching it. "I'm here!" I shout. "I'm right here!"

"I hear you," the voice replies, and I can't tell if I'm going to laugh or cry. "How're you feeling?"

"A lot better now that you're here," I choke out. "What's your name?"

"Jeremy," he says, his voice growing clearer. "Nice to meet you, ma'am."

I finally laugh, though my throat is tight. "Kim is fine. What do you need me to do?"

"Stay where you are," he says. "I think we've found the debris you're trapped under. We'll need to assess the area, shore up anything that needs it, and then we'll start getting you out of there."

"Don't take long, please," I say, and I hate the way my voice breaks. "I'd really like a shower."

"Don't worry, Kim." His voice sounds more distant, and my heart thunders in my chest. "We'll have you out of there in no time."

And then, I'm left in the dark, in silence, ears straining to make out the sounds of the rescue team working on the other side of the concrete slab. I press my hand against it, my palm wet with nervous sweat, and I grit my teeth against the sob rising in my throat.

You've got this, I tell myself. *Almost there. Hold it together a bit longer.*

I turn to Priya. *Any sign of Rivera?*

No, she says. *I think the rescue team scared him off.*

Great. I sigh. *You think they'll get us out of here before the binding breaks?*

She shrugs. *Maybe? It's holding pretty well right now.*

You saw him Turning, though. It won't hold for long.

We both look to the concrete, then back at each other. *Can you reach your knife?* Priya asks.

I pull my knees up to my chest and slip my fingers into my boot. The silver of the handle is cold against my fingers, but it's an awkward position, and when I try to draw the dagger from its sheath, something catches, locking it tight against my leg. After a few fruitless tugs, I slide it back in and shake my head.

Still stuck. I think it may have gotten hit by something when the building came down.

Are you in any pain? Priya hovers her hand over my ankle, and there's a cold sensation against my skin. I shiver. *I'm not sensing anything worse than a bruise.*

It's fine, I agree. *Nothing we can't put off until after we get out of here.*

We sit in silence as we wait for the team to start

working. Other than muffled voices and the occasional scrape of metal or rock, it's quiet on the other side of the concrete.

So far, I've been distracted by either my injuries or Rivera's ghost. Now that neither requires my immediate attention, I want to claw my way out of the rubble. Patience isn't my strong suit, and whatever remnants I've been clinging to have disappeared like Rivera. I'm desperate, anxious. I don't know if Priya can sense it, but she stays silent for the most part, except for quick darting visits to check on the progress of the rescue team.

I'm staring into the darkness above my head, dropping in and out of Second-Sight as a way to keep my mind occupied, when the gravel my feet are resting against shifts. Heart racing, I throw up a shield, preparing myself for another collapse. Instead, something soft and giving brushes against the bottom of my boot, and a voice, no longer muffled, calls to me.

"That you, Detective?"

"Only if your name is Jeremy," I joke, fighting for lightness.

"That'd be it, ma'am."

"Kim." I swallow back relief. "It's just Kim."

"All right, Kim. We're going to clear the rest of this material, and then we'll pull you out. Are you injured? We were told you got a bad knock on the head."

"I'm all right," I say. "Just a bit of a headache."

"Okay. We're going to put a collar on you to be safe.

Should only be a few more minutes."

"Thank you," I say as his hand moves from my foot to the gravel surrounding it.

I move as far out of the way as I can, listening as Jeremy talks to the rest of the team and they carefully remove rubble. After what feels like an eon, light flashes inside my tiny cavity. I blink against it, then squint to make out the face beneath the headlamp.

Jeremy is young, his face stained with dust and his hair covered by a hard hat. His eyes, a dark brown, shine with kindness and when he smiles, his quiet satisfaction is nearly physical in its impact.

"Hey there," he says. "You think you can shimmy your way out of here, or should I pull?"

My voice is thick with unshed tears. "I think I can make it."

"Okay." He backs up, the light from his lamp glancing around the wreckage past the barrier of my feet. "She's coming out!"

My body protests as I move my way to the opening at my feet. I've been almost immobile for hours, and my muscles cramp and ache with every small motion. Slowly, though, I make my painful, stinging way toward freedom.

The rescue team's headlamps coat the remains of the basement in stark, clear light. Though I know I was lucky to not have been crushed outright, it's made all the clearer as I take in the rest of the ruins.

If there's a floor, I can't find it. Everything is

covered in dust and broken concrete. Cracks run through everything. There's a twisted mess of metal pancaked between thick slabs of concrete and steel. It might have been the furnace, judging by the black char marks covering it and the area around it. The space is pitch black outside of the thin beams of the headlamps, but where they glance over damaged steel and concrete, the small space I ended up in feels less like a prison and more like a safe haven.

"Holy shit," I breathe, and Jeremy laughs.

"Yeah, you were lucky. Let's get this collar on you and get you out of here."

I let him wrap the heavy foam collar around my neck, immobilizing it. He gestures for me to go ahead of him.

"Rebekah is going to lead you out of here. I'll be right behind."

A woman who appears to be close to my age nods at me. "It's a bit tight in places, but once we get through the door, it opens up a lot. We'll have you walking out of here in a few minutes."

I try to nod in response, but I'm caught short by the collar. "I'm right behind you," I say instead and start crawling after her.

She's not wrong about the tight fit. There's one section where concrete has narrowed into a passage that I struggle to get through. When the hard surface of the concrete presses against my chest, holding my breath for me, panic rises. I freeze, the primitive part of my brain convinced that I'm going to die here. A strong hand wraps around my wrist, and I raise my eyes to meet Rebekah's.

"You've got this," she says before exerting gentle pressure on my arm. "Just a bit farther."

I bite my lip, plant my feet, and push. With her pulling, I slowly drag through the choke point and tumble into the open space beyond it.

I vaguely recognize it as the hallway that we walked down to get to the boiler room earlier that morning. It looks like a crumpled box now. Drywall is cracked and warped, and wires hang from the ruined ceiling like viscera. Rebekah's headlamp bounces down the hall, and I follow after her, stunned into silence.

She directs me up a set of stairs that look almost normal, only a few cracks in the cinder block walls showing signs of damage. As I walk outside, I wince, my eyes struggling to adjust to even the half-dim light of a cloudy, late afternoon. A cheer rises around me, the gathered crowd watching as I stumble out.

I blink back tears as Jeremy and the rest of the rescue team climb out of the building.

"All clear!" he shouts to someone I can't make out, my vision still blurred. He places his hand gently on my shoulder. "Let's get you to an ambulance. You need to get checked out by a doctor."

I let him guide me away from the building. My legs start to cramp, and I bite my lip against the pain. Someone calls my name, but I can't turn my head to look with the collar on.

Here he comes, Priya says, slightly teasing. *I'm surprised it took him this long.*

I stop and turn my whole body toward the familiar voice and see Cross barreling toward me, his normally tidy hair disheveled and his green eyes wide.

"Kim."

My name is like breath stolen from his lungs. A gust of air ripped from his body. It hits me, and I start to shake as he stills. His approach is slow at first, a hesitant handful of steps that have his feet dragging across the ground. But then he speeds up until he's nearly running. I take a step forward, Jeremy's hand falling from my back, and then Cross's arms are wrapped around me. I shut my eyes and collapse.

He catches me, and my hands scrabble for purchase on the soft fabric of his jacket. I breathe him in, desperate to be closer to him, to have his strength wrapped around me.

"Thank God." He breathes the words into my hair. "If you ever let me sleep in again…"

I laugh, though it comes out as a sob. "I'm kicking you out next time, I promise."

He pulls back and traces his hands over the collar around my neck. "Are you okay? How are you feeling?"

"Fucking tired," I say, covering his hands with my own. I give them a gentle squeeze and push them away, aware of Jeremy nearby and the crowd gathered around the site. "And in desperate need of a shower."

"Detective Cross," Jeremy says, breaking into the moment, "we need to get her looked at."

"Of course," Cross says. He steps back and takes my elbow in his grip, his fingers gentle but firm.

He guides me toward the ambulance, and Jeremy peels off, heading toward a set of white plastic tables where a group of firefighters are gathered.

"You're being a little possessive, don't you think?" I ask.

"Probably," he says as his grip on my elbow gentles. "Can you blame me, though?"

"No," I say, letting myself be possessed, "I can't."

Chapter Twenty-Five

Priya

Kim steps into the back of the ambulance, Riley helping her. His hand only lingers for a beat too long. The careful touch makes me smile, and as the EMT starts asking Kim about her injuries, I float back toward Taka, who's standing near the perimeter of the site, eyeing the circle that Andrea scribed.

She's good, I Send. He doesn't startle at my voice but instead turns his dark, distant eyes toward me, immutable as stone.

Andi is a talented young woman. I have no doubt about her abilities.

Only in mine and Kim's, I say. *You've been avoiding us.*

If he flinches, I can't see it. Turning back to the chalk, he bends down and lets his fingers trail the ground near the circle. *Things have been… hectic lately. It is no reflection on my belief in your abilities, only on the growing need for Burners.*

Really. I scoff. *Let's talk about that growing need. What's going on in Chicago? You know more than you're telling us, and it's tied to Ruth.*

And we will talk when the time is right.

I don't see why now isn't the right time. I gesture toward the building. *We had a ghost Turn in a handful of days. At that rate, time may not be a luxury we can afford anymore.*

When you are ready, he hedges, *we will talk about what I suspect.*

And why do you think we're not ready now? We're not children.

His head snaps up, and I swear his eyes flash white. *You should watch your tone, Priya.*

No. I let power flow into my body, and my hair starts to rise. *I'm tired of waiting, Takashi. We deserve answers.*

He stares at me. Power crackles through the air, tainting it with ozone and anger. Hair whips around me in a black nimbus, and I watch as the skin on my fingers reddens and starts to crack. Taka's eyes burn into me as his hands shift toward the knife I know he keeps in the small of his back. That tentative motion stills, then stops before he turns away from me, dismissive, to continue examining the chalk marks on the ground.

Not now, he says. The words are familiar, but the tone in his voice isn't. It's hesitant, uncertain. *When she is healed and rested. Then, we will talk.*

His shoulders are tight, but when I let the gathered power in my body go, they relax. *No more secrets.*

We will talk.

I nod, though he can't see it, and drift away, circling

back to where Kim sits in the back of the ambulance. The cervical collar has been removed, and there's an IV taped to her arm. I check the bag, frowning when I see it's only saline.

That's all they're giving you? I ask Kim, settling near her.

She sighs. *I'm slightly dehydrated. Cross made them put the bag in, but I would've been fine with Pedialyte or something.*

He cares about you, I say, surprised that he's not in the ambulance with her. *Where'd he go?*

To talk to the firefighter in charge of the scene. He wants to make sure they don't need him for anything else.

With the way he's been making a nuisance of himself all day, I'd be surprised if she doesn't banish him from the site entirely.

Kim smiles. *He was that worried?*

Terrified. I'm surprised his hair hasn't turned white.

Thank you, she Sends after a moment, *for keeping an eye on him. Keeping him calm.*

He cares about you. I was simply doing what I'd want someone to do for me.

She looks at me, brow furrowed. *And you're okay? I can't imagine that it was easy for you, either.*

I'm… I trail off, not sure what to say. My fear was a living thing, a writhing, twisting snake in my gut. *It was a lot today.*

Do you want to talk about it?

I laugh. *You never want to talk about things.*

She hunches in on herself and buries one hand in her dirty hair to rub against the part of her scalp that was split open by a rogue piece of concrete earlier. *I think I'm going to want to talk about this.*

It was terrifying, I say, trying to temper my honesty with comfort. *I love you. It wasn't easy seeing you hurt and being unable to help.*

You helped. Her voice is quiet but firm. *I wouldn't have made it without you.*

Maybe, but I think you're stronger than you think you are.

She smiles. *I learned that from you, too.*

Movement on the edge of the crowd draws our attention. Kim's head lifts, and she pulls her hand from her hair to lay it on top of the IV in the crook of her arm.

I talked to Taka, I say. *He's going to talk to us once you start feeling better.*

She sighs and lets her head loll back, her eyes closing as relief floods her face. *Finally. What'd you tell him?*

I may have threatened him, I say, embarrassed, *a little bit.*

Well done. She laughs. *As soon as this bag is empty, I'm getting out of here. I don't care if they want to send me to the hospital—I'm going home, taking a shower, and passing out.*

As I laugh, the crowd still gathered around the site parts. Officer Cooper is pushing his way through the cordon, one of his arms in a sling and his uniform jacket tossed over his shoulders. As he reaches the ambulance, taking in Kim's dust- and blood-covered body, his face pales.

And that's when it all goes to hell.

I hear it coming before I see it. A low roar that grows, emanating from the bowels of the building's ruins. The bass of it thrums through me, shaking my incorporeal form with growing waves of power. Dust swirls, wind whipping through the parking lot and sending gravel and debris skipping over the tarmac to lash against the crowd gathered around the site. A few people turn their heads, their faces twisted in confusion, and they cover their eyes as a blast of red-black power sweeps over them. They can't see it, can't interact with it, but it still sends them stumbling back. Cross, who's standing at the command center, turns toward the building, eyes wide and power crackling between his fingers.

Darkness rises from the center of the building in a roiling mass. It creaks and snaps, bending in awkward, unnatural shapes as it grows larger and larger until it hovers over the wreckage of steel and concrete like a storm cloud. The figure hints at humanity, though its size and the twisted, wrecked shape of it say otherwise. As it raises its head, its eyes—black and writhing with white beneath—turn toward Cooper and Kim, and its broken, bloated mouth splits open into a grin.

"Oh shit," Kim says, and then she's up, IV ripped from her arm as she shoves Cooper back toward the ambulance while yelling for Taka.

He runs toward her, a binding forming between his hands in a ball of light that he throws forward with a shout. It slams into the ghost, sending a shower of sparks into the air as the binding tries to wrap its way around the creature's body. It tilts its head down, neck twisted into right angles, before brushing at the binding and extinguishing the light with its broken fingers.

Justice. Its voice booms in my head. I shrink back, covering my ears with my hands, though it won't do anything to stop the noise. *Is mine.*

The creature lunges forward, one of its hands reaching for Kim. I dart in front of her as she throws up a shield. It barely covers her, Taka, and Cooper. Pouring power into the thin barrier of light, I reach for Taka and Kim. His energy darts into me, and I funnel it into the shield as it grows before looping it back into Kim's reserves. A moment later, Claire appears next to me and adds her strength to the group's.

Is that who I think it is? I ask Kim, her teeth gritted as she holds steady under the Turned ghost's hunting fingers.

Yeah, it's Rivera.

What made him Turn again?

No idea, but we're gonna need help keeping him contained.

I grimace. *On it.* Turning my attention away from the ghost, I search for Riley and Andrea.

Thankfully, they're already on top of things. Riley is crouched on the ground near the circle sketched around the site, a Swiss Army knife in his hand. He drags the tip of it across his palm, blood blooming red and wet against his skin, and he presses it into the chalk.

The circle leaps into life. Rays of energy shoot into the sky, then arc over the parking lot like buttresses in a cathedral. The beams meet above the parking lot, their ends blending together until the places where they join are indistinguishable from the rest of the protective barrier. A ripple moves out across the ground, a low shiver of energy that sends my hair whipping away from my face. Riley gasps, his body shuddering, but he keeps his palm planted on the ground as the power races from his body into the circle.

Distracted by the sudden flash of light and power, the Turned ghost lifts its head and reaches for the barrier. When its fingers brush against it, Riley curls into himself, muscles straining as energy pours out of him. Sparks fly, golden and bright, and the ghost pulls back, its slow and ponderous movements in sharp contrast to the scream of pain that leaps from its broken mouth.

Hurts, it moans before turning its attention back to Kim and Taka. *No more.*

There aren't many people within the protective circle, but the few who are have their eyes locked on the ghost, bodies paralyzed by fear.

"Banks!" Kim shouts, and Andrea's head turns her way. "Get these people out of here!"

Her dark hair bobs as she nods, and she rushes forward, arms waving to get their attention. "You have to leave!" she shouts, and slowly, they stumble away from her and toward the police cordon. "Get to the street. You'll be safe there."

"Whatever you say," one of the firefighters shouts, his hard hat pushed back on his head as he ushers other people away from the Turned ghost. "Good luck!"

As emergency personnel run away from the building, the ghost brings its attention to them. Its hand, the broken fingers and bones of it encased in decomposing flesh, drags across the ground. Slowly, gravel and debris gather in the wrecked palm, growing until they form a low wall of rock. The first firefighter it crashes into stumbles but keeps her feet as she dodges away. The second isn't so lucky. He crashes to the ground, arms stretched in front of him, fingers scrabbling against the tarmac as his legs and hips are covered. The ghost's hand sweeps over his head, his scream cut short, and when it moves on, there's only a low, shifting pile of rock where the man once was.

Andrea runs over and starts digging him out, but my attention is snagged when the ghost reaches for Kim and Taka again. With its hand wrapped around the shield, it squeezes. Electric pain consumes my body as power is ripped from me. I'm momentarily stunned by it, but as the haze clears from my mind, I race toward the creature, energy gathered in a ball between my hands. I send it crashing into the thinnest part of the creature's wrist, and its whole hand shivers before it releases the shield.

Why? it asks as it moves toward me, its hand grasping blindly in the air. *This is justice.*

Confused, I hurry to Kim's side. Taka's and her combined shield is still bright and strong, keeping the ghost away from Cooper, who is trapped inside the ambulance with an EMT. *What's it talking about?*

I'm not entirely sure, she says. *We'll figure it out after we get rid of this thing.*

The Turned ghost growls, and it reaches for the

ambulance again. Claire flares her power, sending the questing, broken fingers back again. A scream erupts from its throat, and red-black power washes over all of us in a crushing wave. Kim bares her teeth as the caustic energy tears at the shield. Cursing under his breath in Japanese, Taka falls to a knee, a piece of chalk held between his bloodless fingers. He frantically scribes symbols on the ground. Tossing his chalk aside before grabbing his knife from the sheath on his back, he tears a vicious cut through the delicate skin of his inner arm, and as blood splashes onto the sigils and runes on the ground before him, the shield strengthens, then steadies.

"Thank you," Kim pants. She sways on her feet and her face pales. Reaching behind her for the step into the ambulance, she falls back, landing hard on the metal bumper. "What does it want?"

Justice! The creature reaches forward with both of its hands and grabs the ambulance. While corporeal enough to be seen, it isn't fully manifested, and its fingers slide through the metal before sweeping over the shield and darting away with a flash of light. *Revenge!*

"Why would it want revenge against you?" Taka asks, turning to Kim. "What did you do?"

"Nothing," she says. Her voice is weak, but it's still rich with anger. "Goddammit, what are we missing?"

Inside the ambulance, Cooper's face is white and slack. His uninjured arm is by his side, his hand resting on his gun. As I watch his fingers tighten on the holster, something in my mind clicks.

Kim, I say in a rush. *It's Cooper.*

She turns tired eyes my way as the ghost makes another fumbling swipe at the ambulance. This time, the whole vehicle shakes, the ghost's overly large fingers crumpling the aluminum body. Cooper hunches down, his hand falling away from his gun.

Now isn't the time, Priya, she says before sending more power into the shield. *We need to distract Rivera and get Cooper and the EMT out of here.*

The EMT's gone, I Send, noting the now-open driver's side door of the ambulance. Cooper's headed in the same direction, stumbling over a stretcher that's been knocked onto its side and the various medical equipment now strewn around the interior of the ambulance. *And Cooper's about to be. Shit, you've got to stop him.*

We've got a bigger problem to deal with right now, she says, her voice strained as she fights to keep the Turned ghost's hand from crushing her and Taka.

I groan, annoyed that she's not getting it. *Rivera attacked when Cooper showed up. He's obsessed with getting revenge against his killer. Put two and two together for God's sake.*

The realization shakes through her like a blow. Eyes wide, she looks at Cooper's back as he scrambles into the front of the ambulance.

Shit. She freezes. *He's the killer. He's the dirty cop.*

CHAPTER TWENTY-SIX

RILEY

The ambulance rocks on its suspension as the Turned ghost's massive hand wraps around the metal frame and squeezes. Kim and Taka both flinch, their bodies straining as they continue to power the thin shield of light wrapped around themselves and the vehicle. Priya, her hair flying around her face in a wild mess, looks at me, eyes wide.

Riley, you've got to stop him!

I won't let him through, I Send back, fighting to push more power into the protective circle, *but Kim and Taka are going to have to figure out how to Burn him. I don't know what's going to happen if he tries to test the boundary.*

Not the ghost, Priya shouts. *Cooper!*

Confused, I watch as the man in question stumbles out of the ambulance and runs toward the perimeter.

No. The voice in my mind is like the deep rumble of stone against stone. *Justice will be mine.*

The Turned ghost reaches for Cooper, its broken and bloody fingers moving through the air as if in slow motion. Cooper, his eyes wide and white, stares at it over his shoulder, and though he trips over the ground, he stays on his feet and barrels through the glowing perimeter.

When the ghost's hand crashes into it, power pours out of me like a tap turned on full. It hurts, my whole body suddenly on fire, all of my nerves screaming as energy drains in a dizzying rush. I want to scream, but I can't breathe. All I can do is press my hands into the ground and fight to stay conscious.

The ghost pulls back, sparks flying, and I gasp, my vision dimming as it backs away. It opens its mouth, and thick, white maggots start falling to the ground like vomit.

Not again, it moans, its fingers skating across the ground as it tests another section of the barrier. Pain lances through me, and I fall onto my elbows, forehead pressed into the unforgiving ground as my body shakes and quivers. *You will pay.*

As my vision narrows into a darkening tunnel, I wonder when Andrea's fail-safe will trip. I don't understand how my power feeds the circle or how it feeds back into me, but surely unconsciousness will shut it off.

Someone yells my name. It's tinny and small, and when I turn my head to find where it's coming from, I fall to my side. My hand slips from the chalk lines. Blood smears on the tarmac, red and slick. The ghost claws at the barrier. Flesh falls from its fingers before melting into the ground. Then that vision dims, and darkness digs its way into my mind, drawing me down.

My chest splinters like ice.

Power, hot and scalding, explodes out of me in a golden wave. My back bows up, and I writhe against the ground as a burning cold flays me alive. It eats away at my skin and muscles, burns its piercing way through my chest to pour onto the ground and mix with my blood. My eyes roll back in my head, and everything is washed away in white and gold and red and black.

A roaring silence. It echoes and thumps and suffocates. Something warm and soft like fur slides through my fingers. All around, darkness. An unending, starless night sky. I drift through it, mind distant and numb, as pain rocks through me like waves against a shore. Lapping, gentle touches send agony coursing through me. I fade with each ebb and flow until I float away on it, my breaths even and slow.

There's a low, steady beat in the distance. My eyes slide open, and I watch as my body rolls onto its front, then stands. Its knees tremble. Its steps are unsteady. As it moves, its motions grow more confident. Hands turn palm up, then down, fingers spreading wide. Someone laughs before my body's hand presses against the center of its chest. Pain sweeps me away like a riptide, and the hand falls away. The palm is burnt in the shape of a circle quartered by a cross.

"Of course," my voice hisses.

There's a roar and red-black power washes through the void in a wave that warps the darkness. The thing controlling my body takes a step back and laughs. Still laughing, it raises my arms and power gathers between its outstretched palms. The ball of energy is a swirling mass, a riotous mix of red and black and gold. It's small at first, about the size of a baseball, but it continues growing until it's nearly three feet across. The heat of it blisters my palms, though I can't feel it. There's a sweet smell like burning sugar.

I look up. Though the world is still dark, still that endless, lightless black sky, I am surrounded by the dead, vague human shapes that turn the darkness around me gray. All around is a glowing circle of white. Twisting lines tangle their way through the ground like vines over a forest floor. They pulse in time with the distant, steady thump that echoes in my ears.

In the center of it all is the Turned ghost. I look at it, my motions sluggish, as if I were underwater. It's somehow *less* in this hollowness we're trapped in. Though it still towers over me, its body is thin and emaciated. Where there had been bloated flesh, there's only spindly arms and legs, and a torso that's caved in and covered with paper-like skin. Its eyes, black and writhing, are locked on the ball of power held before me. Something like understanding, like fear, flashes in its expression, but that's lost as the energy shoots from between my hands toward it.

The power slams into the creature's body, clinging to its form. Though the Turned ghost slaps its broken hands against the burning light, it doesn't go out. Instead, it sticks to the ghost's discolored skin, coating the creature's fingers in shifting red, black, and gold. Crackling energy crawls over its body, wrapping it in a beautiful, awful stain. Bones crack beneath the pressure, and as the energy coats its throat, then claws its way into the ghost's broken mouth, a voice screams.

I think it might be mine.

Forcing myself out of the thick, cloying fog I'm trapped in, I wrench my way toward my body. Something's clinging to the center of my chest, a darkness that's thicker than the rest, and I grab at it with fingers that pass through my clothes to scratch my skin.

No! There's a wrenching sensation, and when I look down, blood coats my hands. It's red and bright, and it pulses in time with the world around us. With my heart.

I don't know what I'm fighting against, but I tear into it, teeth bared, as I try to wrestle it from my body. It twists and writhes, its body slick and insubstantial. Though I try, I can't get a tight grip on it. It slips through my fingers, but as it does, its hold on my body loosens. Since I can't rip it free, I press myself tighter to my own skin, using the creature's momentum to force it away. It desperately tries to hang on, imperceptible claws that cut through to the bone, but then it falls away, unable to keep hold with me in between it and my body.

With a shout, I fall back into myself.

The darkness disappears in a rush, and I'm left standing on unsteady feet in the middle of a parking lot, air whipping around me in a tornado as golden power coats the ground around me and the body of the Turned ghost clawing at the barrier. Only now, instead of trying to reach its victim, it's fighting to escape. Its fingers throw sparks as they glance off the barrier, but I don't feel it anymore. Instead, there's a numbness that's bone deep. My body feels like it's fallen asleep, and as pins and needles explode across my skin, the ghost screams.

I don't want to die, it moans as the golden light finishes wrapping its way around its face, cutting off its voice. The silence left behind is deafening. It claws at its throat and face, then turns its whirling, gray eyes toward me.

First one lumbering step, then another. Its arms stretch forward, and I stumble back as it collapses to the ground, fingers outstretched toward me. They slam into the ground, and I feel it ripple through my legs. The creature's body explodes into thousands of wriggling grubs, each one coated in gold. They thrash around my feet, and I fall back onto the ground. Maggots explode under my body, leaving white and gold smears across my clothes. I frantically swipe at them, trying to scrape off the soft pulp of their bodies. They fade, sinking into the tarmac until there's no sign of their ghostly bodies. All that's left is the soft glow of the barrier around us.

And Kim, Taka, and Andrea, their eyes wide with fear and locked on me, lying sprawled on the ground.

"Did we get him?" I croak out, and everything goes dark.

Chapter Twenty-Seven

Kim

My hair is wet, and the borrowed scrubs I'm in are an odd mix of scratchy from cheap detergent and soft from being washed a million times. Faded into some indeterminate shade of blue, they're slightly too big, but considering the ruined state of my own clothes, it's better than nothing. At least they're clean. My feet, which are up and resting on the edge of a hospital bed, are cradled in thick, fuzzy socks that Andrea found in the gift shop downstairs.

"Pretty sure they're for new moms," she said before handing them to me, "but I figured you'd like them."

They're bright pink and covered in tiny unicorns and hearts.

I desperately want to hate them, but they're the softest damn things I've ever worn in my life. I curl my toes, letting their downy softness tickle my skin and distract me from the body in the bed.

Cross is pale. There's an IV in his arm, the bright red light of a pulse-ox monitor clipped to his finger. He's been asleep since they brought him in. From what

Priya's been able to tell, that's all it is. No concussion, no brain damage, just complete and total exhaustion.

I keep hoping he'll shift, that his eyes will open, and I'll see their normal, green hue. When he turned toward me, his body swaying as the remains of Rivera's ghost faded into the ground, his eyes were black.

Black and red.

The last time I saw that color in his gaze was when Baker possessed him and nearly killed me, and I scarred Cross's chest with a Burner's symbol. It's still there, a low, soft glow of golden-white light that is a reassuring brightness in the dimness of the hospital room.

He's going to be okay, Priya Sends. She appears at the foot of his bed, then lays her hand over my feet. *Once he gets enough rest, he'll be fine.*

You're sure about that? I ask, kicking my feet from the edge of the bed to the floor. I pull my chair closer, the uneven legs scraping across the floor, and take his limp hand in mine. His hospital admission band shifts on his wrist, and I push it farther up his arm to press my fingers against his steady pulse. *He might recover from whatever happened back there, but how do you know that something worse isn't coming?*

She sighs and rests her hand over mine. *I don't. But we knew that something was happening to him before today, Kim.*

I didn't think it would be… I swallow back fear. *We have to do something.*

She nods but doesn't say anything else.

I'm still processing what happened before. One

second, Cross was lying on the ground, his body sprawled near the protective barrier around the destroyed office building. The next, golden energy was flooding the parking lot, so powerful it wiped away our shield and sent Priya and Claire flying. And in the center of it, Cross, his arms cradling a ball of energy so large and bright, it hurt to look at it, and his eyes as black and cold as polished jet. He unleashed that power with hardly a thought, sent it crashing into the Turned ghost with an ease that chilled me.

He watched Rivera's ghost Burn, and he smiled.

You hear anything about Cooper? Priya asks, breaking me out of my thoughts.

Yeah. He didn't get far, but he's lawyered up. I'm hoping we'll have enough from my Readings and the physical evidence to catch him. Martinez is already working on getting a warrant for Cooper's blood.

John Cooper, but everyone knew him as Jack. Priya shakes her head. *Smart of him to use a nickname on the job.*

Not smart enough, though. Once Martinez finds the gunman, he's done.

When are you talking to the sketch artist?

Walker said he should be here in about an hour. It's not much time to recover, but it needs to happen. I yawn and rest my elbows on the bed, Cross's hand held between my own. *I'm a little jealous. He's leaving me with all the paperwork.*

Priya smiles, but it's weak. *Like he won't go over all of it once he wakes up.*

I'll make some typos, give him something to look forward to. I press my mouth against his knuckles and close my eyes. *He's going to be fine.*

He's going to be fine.

I fall into Second-Sight and stare at the bright mark in the center of his chest. My mark. A circle quartered by a cross with one arm longer than the rest. It shimmers and shines, warm and familiar and comforting.

And in the center, a small patch of darkness like a starless night sky.

"Kim."

I drop Cross's hand and sit up, eyes opening as I turn toward the voice.

Taka stands in the doorway. For the first time in my life, he looks old. His wrinkles stand out, and his hair is still streaked with dust from the site. He walks into the room and falls into another chair, his body collapsing in on itself as he stares at Cross, unconscious between us.

"I think"—his voice is hoarse and unsteady—"that there are some things we need to talk about."

The muscles in my body tense and I fight the urge to clench my hands into fists.

"I'm listening."

And he begins to speak.

Glossary of Terms

Medium — A person possessing the ability to interact and communicate with the afterlife and spirits of deceased people. Mediums make up about 0.2 percent of the population, depending on the area. They Bond with ghosts who have yet to Turn as the final step of their training, which increases their power and stops the ghost from Turning.

Turning — When a ghost loses their sense of reality and becomes dangerous to living people. After Turning, ghosts may cause damage to property, as well as people.

Affinity — The specialized skill set a Medium possesses. The seven Affinities, from most common to least, are Burner, Reader, Healer, Speaker, Shaker, Seer, Passenger.

Burner — This is the most common type of Medium. They can speak with and exorcise ghosts and usually work in criminal justice or as independent contractors.

Reader — Gains memories and emotions from physical objects. Clarity of images and depth of information is dependent on their power and how long they're in contact with the item. The longer they spend trying to find out information from something, the better it is, but there is a limit to what they can discover. Most items will not trigger anything when a Reader is in contact with them, but some items that have a strong psychic aura will cause them to fall into a vision without warning. Second most common type of Medium.

Healer — Possesses healing abilities and can view internal structures. They are regarded with extreme respect and sought out regularly by hospitals and convalescent homes. They tend to be very caring individuals, who form significant emotional bonds with the people they trust and love. The strength of the Medium determines how severe of an injury or illness they can heal. Third most common type.

Speaker — Can communicate telepathically with other Mediums and people who have a predisposition for the supernatural. Work with Burners and Readers regularly. Also tend to work in special forces or the military due to their ability to Speak to people. The strength of the Medium determines how far and how many people they can Speak with at a time. Fourth most common type.

Shaker — Can move things and people without physically touching them. The weight of the item or person they can move is determined by the Medium's power. They tend to work in dangerous construction jobs, like underwater drilling and high-rise construction and repair. They are also commonly found working in disaster areas, especially earthquakes, as support teams. Fifth most common type

Seer — Can see into the future or past. The length of time into the future or past and the clarity of what they See is based on their inherent power. Generally work in the financial, military, or political sector. Sixth most common type.

Passenger — Can possess people for brief moments. Very little is known about this Affinity as it is so uncommon. They have been steadily declining in numbers since the early 1800s. Almost no Mediums of this type are alive currently. Seventh most common type.

Second-Sight — The specialized vision that Mediums use to view and interact with elements of the afterlife. Said to appear as a brightly lit outline of the living world.

Sending — When a Medium or ghost shares a memory or thought with another Medium or ghost. Used as a form of communication for Mediums and their partner ghosts, as well as Speakers when communicating with other Mediums.

Circle — A circle written in chalk used by Mediums to do various things, such as Burning a ghost or Seeing something that happened previously in a location. The function is determined by the sigils and runes used to construct the circle. Powered by the blood of a Medium, otherwise inactive. Will completely disappear after being used.

Runes — Arcane marks that describe the nature of things. Used in circles to describe what the circle is supposed to effect.

Sigils — Arcane marks that link runes together and focus arcane energy in circles. Directs and channels energy in circles.

Wards — Sets of sigils and runes used outside of a circle to protect an area from entry or exit. Generally used on Mediums' homes to stop malevolent or unknown ghosts from entering. Can also be used to stop a ghost from leaving an area.

ACKNOWLEDGEMENTS

Speaker, out of all of the books in *The Affinity Series*, was a struggle. I know I say this in every Acknowledgements section I write, but this time, it was truer than ever before. This book started with a single scene – Kim, standing in the basement of a building, only to be caught in a gas explosion.

That was it.

Honestly, the finished product is better than I expected. Parts of the plot fell into place as I wrote or came to me after talking about elements of the story with friends, family, and colleagues. Without their help, I can say with complete and utter honestly that this book would not exist.

Continued thanks to the members of the Indianapolis Police Department who allow me to bug them with weird questions at all hours of the day and night: Officers Nicholas Gallico and Frank Miller, and retired Officer Michael O'Connor.

My husband is my rock and my cheerleader. He may not understand exactly why I do this, but he supports me 100% and I'd be lost without him. We celebrated 10 years of marriage this May, and I cannot wait for the next decade with him by my side.

Michael, Jennifer, and Susan: I know we didn't meet while I was working on this book, but your voices were in my head as I went. Every time I started a sentence with I, followed by another sentence starting with I, I could hear all three of you shouting at me. So, thank you for breaking my brain, but in the best way possible.

There are not enough words in the English language to explain how amazing my editor, Nikki Busch, continues to be. I dropped this book on Nikki at basically the last second, before I'd even finished writing the draft, and she not only fit me into her schedule, she got it back to me ahead of schedule with thorough, competent, and insightful feedback. I have been absolutely blessed with her help on all of my books, and I owe her more than I can say.

And, as always, I save the best for last: thank you, fans of *The Affinity Series*. As long as you're out there and Kim, Priya, and Riley are talking to me, I will keep putting these books out. I've had the joyous opportunity to speak with some of you at conventions or on social media, and every time, it's incredible. Having people approach me with enthusiasm and excitement about my characters and world will never get old.

Shaker, the next book in the series, is still brewing in my mind. Obviously, you're not the only ones waiting to find out just what Taka has to say. If you want to get updates on its progress or just see how I'm doing, feel free to follow me on Twitter (@p1013) or follow *The Affinity Series* on Facebook.

Thank you all, again, so much.

J. S.

ABOUT THE AUTHOR

J. S. Lenore was born and raised in the suburbs of Chicago. She attended Elgin High School, graduating within the top ten of her class. She majored in Japanese Studies at Earlham College and graduated with honors before getting her Masters in Teaching, also from Earlham College. She started creative writing at a young age, mainly writing fanfiction, but did not find much success until after graduation. In 2013, writing under the handle p1013, J. S. Lenore posted her first fanfiction for MTV's *Teen Wolf*. This story, titled *The Full Moon Like Blood*, and others gained a moderate following. In the same year, she decided to branch out into original fiction, writing the rough draft of *Burner* during National Novel Writing Month. She is currently working on the fifth book in The Affinity Series, *Shaker*.

J. S. Lenore currently lives in Indianapolis with her husband, two children, one cat, one dog, and zero ghosts.